Contents

The Orient Express

She worked at the Orient Express — no, not the luxury train — a Chinese restaurant in the suburbs of Newcastle. Colored paper lanterns sagged in the doorway, their once-bright reds dulled by years of grease and dust. They glowed faintly above the plastic strips that slapped together whenever someone came or went, cloudy and warped, meant to keep flies out but never quite managing. Inside, the air was thick and unmoving. No air conditioning, just the smell of fried oil and jasmine tea clinging to the walls. The tables stayed sticky no matter how much she wiped, and the floor tugged softly at every step, as though the place wanted to trap its visitors.

There was a rhythm to the evenings, a slow churn that began before sunset and found its groove once the street outside turned to black glass. The fluorescent tubes hummed, one of them stuttering now and then as if it had a cough. A lacquered lucky cat by the till waved its paw in a tired loop, battery nearly done, the gesture more stubborn than cheerful. Chopsticks in paper sleeves stood like a picket fence in a cloudy plastic cup. Beside them, takeaway menus lived in a sagging stack, corners curled, the glossy photos sun-faded and too red — sweet and sour pork the color of traffic lights, greens that had never existed in nature.

She moved between the counter and the dining room with a damp cloth and a spray bottle that smelled vaguely of lemons, or at least of something that promised the memory of lemons. Spray, wipe, stick. Spray, wipe, stick. The tables shone without becoming clean, a drizzle of dried sauce clinging to a groove in the laminate like blood in a shallow cut. She prised it up with a fingernail, victorious and faintly disgusted.

Regulars took their usual places without looking at menus. A man with a newspaper ordered special fried rice and a pot of tea. A pair of high-school girls shared honey chicken and whispered over a dog-eared teen magazine, their laughter fizzing and dying whenever the owner walked past. A toddler in a pilled cardigan banged a plastic spoon on the edge of a bowl until the spoon surrendered and skittered to the floor. She retrieved it, smiled automatically at the mother's mouthed apology, and went to fetch another.

The owner's voice rarely carried; his presence did. He arrived in doorways with steam wrapped around him like a cloak, the clang of the wok preceding him, the squeal of shoes on grease-polished tile. He clicked his tongue — *tch tch tch* — and pointed, a swift edit to the room's composition: a nod toward the stack of containers that wanted restocking, a frown at the card reader that needed paper, a quick chop of his hand to launch a delivery driver back through the strips. He seemed to appear wherever the heat was worst, his forehead shining, the rag over his shoulder darkening in stages through the night.

She watched the till accept another crumpled note, the cash drawer yawning like a bored mouth. The card reader hiccuped and spat a ribbon of paper. She tore it off and flattened it with her palm. Her own name lurked somewhere at the edges of the night — she could feel it the way one feels a draft without seeing the door open — but the room used *girl* when it needed her. The word floated from table to table and she answered to it.

At the tea station, the kettle snapped off. She poured water into a dented pot, jasmine rising like a held breath. Steam brushed her face, briefly washing her clean of oil and questions. She refilled glasses, caught the girls' chatter about brothers and parties, and felt a pang for a life where the past was certain, where you knew who you belonged to.

Adopted, she had grown up loved but always aware of a missing thread. That absence had followed her into adulthood, a hollow space where family history should have been. When she'd finally searched for her birth mother, the envelope came heavy in her hands, holding both a name and a death certificate. A door opening and slamming shut in the same breath. The memory still hollowed her out, even as she turned back to wipe the counter.

Outside, neon signs bled onto the footpath as boys skidded by, laughter thin against the night. She drifted through the room polite in three directions at once.

When her break came, it arrived the way all small mercies do — quietly, without ceremony. The owner materialized at the pass, *tch tch tch*, and angled his chin toward the back door. She nodded, set the cloth down, wiped her hands on her apron, and slid along the narrow corridor that ran beside the fridges. A mop leaned in the corner, water clouded and still. The staff calendar near the back door bore names and arrows that meant little unless you lived inside the puzzle; her own name, when she found it, was written faintly, the pencil pressed too softly, as if even the letters were unsure of their right to be there.

She pushed through the rear door into the alley, and the air at once felt like movement — not cooler, exactly, but looser, as if it remembered how to travel. The night smelled of wet concrete, old cabbage from a bin someone hadn't tied properly, and, faintly, rain that might arrive by morning if it felt like it. She leaned against the wall, tipped her head back, and closed her eyes.

From her pocket she shook a single clove cigarette free of its crumpled packet, the paper soft and a little yellowed at the edges. She struck a match against the brick, cupped the flame with her hand, and watched it flare — small sun, small warmth — before the tip took. The first drag drew sweetness and spice onto her tongue, a breath that cut clean through the film the restaurant left behind. Smoke curled upward, thin and pale, then flattened under the weight of the heat before drifting away.

She exhaled, counted to five, and let the night start to speak.

The glow from the cigarette tip pulsed faintly in the dark, a firefly with nowhere urgent to be. She let the smoke sit in her lungs until it bit, then released it slowly, watching the curl dissolve into the night. The clove's sweetness clung to her lips, coating the back of her throat, leaving a sting that felt almost clean compared to the grease-heavy air of the kitchen.

The plastic strips at the front door clattered, muffled by the alley's walls. Footsteps followed, deliberate but unhurried. She didn't turn; she already knew who it was.

The boy came into view, black coat trailing like smoke, his cheekbones cutting pale lines under the stray light of a security lamp. He moved with the grace of someone who had never stumbled, as though even cracked concrete rearranged itself to suit him.

"Got a spare?" he asked, voice low.

She tapped the crumpled packet against her palm until another cigarette slipped out. He took it, pinched it between long fingers, and leaned close when she offered the flame. For a moment, his face was lit from below, skeletal in its beauty, shadows carved deeper by the matchlight. He drew in a breath, ember flaring, and exhaled a plume that smelled of spice and faint sweetness. The smoke hung between them, a small veil, before the alley swallowed it.

"You're working again," he said, the words more observation than question.

"Always." She flicked ash into the gutter.

The quiet settled around them. In it, she could hear the fridge compressor vibrating through the back wall, the drip of a leaky pipe, the faint high whine of the street's lone mosquito making its claim. She wanted to tell him about the envelope — how it had arrived with both her birth mother's name and her death certificate, a door opening and slamming shut at once. She wanted to tell him how she still lay awake wondering why her mother had given her up, what the story was behind that absence, and whether love had played any part in it at all. She wanted to tell him what it was to live with that silence in her blood, to feel the shape of a family she could never touch.

But she didn't speak. She never did.

Instead, she studied the smoke that curled from the boy's lips. He seemed carved from it, ephemeral and solid all at once, the clove cigarette just another ritual in a life full of them. Finally, he dropped the stub, ground it beneath his heel, and looked at her. "Come on," he said. "Let's walk."

She hesitated only long enough to finish hers. The clove burned down to the paper, tasting of sweetness gone bitter. She let it fall, crushing it under her shoe until the ember smeared into nothing. Then she followed.

They slipped from the alley to the street, and the town opened around them. Neon hummed above takeaway shops, bleeding red and blue across the wet pavement. The laundromat's sign buzzed faintly, half its letters dark. A fish-and-chip shop two doors down had closed early, grease still staining the air. Kids on BMX bikes cut sharp arcs under the amber wash of a streetlamp, their laughter carrying until it broke against the row of shuttered storefronts.

They passed a video rental store with posters sun-bleached to ghosts, sleeves of forgotten films leaning in the window. The scent of fried batter gave way to damp concrete, then to nothing but night. A bus rattled by on the main road, its windows a row of faces staring without seeing, lit briefly before the darkness swallowed them again.

She walked beside the boy, listening to the rhythm of his steps. Even that sounded different: measured, graceful, like each stride had been rehearsed long before tonight. She tucked her hands into her apron pockets, wishing she had something to say, something that wouldn't sound ordinary in his presence. But the silence between them didn't demand filling. It spread out comfortably, like the smoke they'd left behind.

Her thoughts returned to the envelope, to the name and the death certificate pressed together like a cruel trick. She wanted to ask *why me?* — why she had been given up, how her mother had made that choice — but the words always shrank in her throat. People would think she was ungrateful. She had a family, she was loved; wasn't that enough? Still, the question gnawed, unanswered and unanswerable.

The boy walked just ahead, shoulders tilted as if he carried his own secrets. For a moment, she imagined he might already know her question, might even hold the answer. But he didn't turn, and she didn't ask.

The streets narrowed, houses leaning close, paint peeling, curtains drawn. A dog barked from somewhere unseen, a harsh sound that cut short. Jasmine clung to old fences, releasing its scent into the night air. The air was heavier here and tinged with damp earth.

When they reached the cemetery, it was not with ceremony but inevitability. The iron gate sagged, one hinge rusted, ivy curling like desperate fingers around the bars. The girl paused, watching the boy slip easily through, the hem of his coat brushing weeds that reached toward him like supplicants. She followed, the clatter of her shoes loud against the gravel path.

The graveyard opened before them — tilted stones, names eroded into moss, angels cracked at the wings. Grass grew high in patches, brittle stalks bending under their weight. The air felt colder here, though the night had not changed.

The boy stopped at a stone that slanted slightly to one side, its carving faint but still legible. He reached into his coat and withdrew an apple, pale under the thin light of the moon.

A blade flashed as he cut it clean in half. One piece he placed on the stone, the other he pressed into her palm.

"Look," he said, tilting his chin toward the star of seeds revealed inside. She stared at it, the shape sharp and impossibly simple, and then his voice spilled into the space between them — words naming her mother, her loss, the hollow questions she never dared speak aloud.

Her breath caught. How could he know? She had never told anyone, not even the people who raised her. The need to ask *why me?* was a secret she carried like shame, one she thought would make her sound pathetic, ungrateful. Yet here he was, pulling it into the open as though he'd reached straight into her chest.

Her thumb pressed into the flesh until a bead of juice welled up. She wanted to scoff, to laugh at the absurdity of standing in a half-forgotten graveyard with a boy who looked like he belonged to shadows, waiting for fruit to give her answers. But she couldn't.

He placed his half carefully on the grave, bowing his head as though presenting an offering. Then he slipped the blade away and began to speak.

The words were nothing she recognized. Not Latin from hymns or prayers, not the mumbled lines from the Bible her adopted mother had tried to press on her. These words rolled like stones in water, heavy and round, some sharp at the edges. They seemed older than the cracked angels leaning over them. His voice was low, steady, and the air seemed to lean in to catch it.

Her skin prickled. The night felt thicker, the grass brushing her ankles colder. The silence of the graveyard deepened, not emptier but *watching*.

She closed her eyes. Behind her lids she saw light, thin and wavering, like a candle guttering in wind. She thought of the envelope, the way it had given her both a name and a death certificate, opening a door only to slam it shut. The questions never stopped: Who did she look like? Did they share the same interests, the same crooked smile? What stories lived in her bloodline, what ancestors shaped her? Those things made people whole, gave them a mirror to see themselves in. For her, they formed a puzzle with half the pieces missing — and now she knew she would never get to ask the one person who might have answered.

Then came the voice. Not his. Not hers. A woman's voice, far away and close enough to breathe against her ear.

I loved you.

Her eyes snapped open. She staggered back, almost dropping the apple.

I was only a child myself.

The sound wasn't like speech, not fully. It bent the air, pressing through the rustle of leaves, carried on the breath of the night.

"They made me let you go," the voice said, trembling, urgent. *"I never wanted to."*

Her chest burned. She wanted to throw the apple, to claw the words into something more solid. She forced sound into her throat. "Who made you?" she whispered. "Why—why didn't you—"

The air shifted. The candle-light in her mind flared, then dimmed.

So young. No choice. I wanted—

The voice fractured, split like glass under strain. She clutched the apple half tighter, juice running sticky across her palm, but the sound was slipping already, retreating.

"Wait," she begged. "Just tell me — did you think of me? Even once?"

The silence that followed was so long she thought the connection had broken. Then, faintly, as though from the bottom of a well:

Every day.

The words wrapped her, warm and unbearable. She gasped, apple falling from her hand. It struck the ground, splitting open, seeds shining like small black eyes.

And then it was gone. The air loosened. The graveyard became only stone and weeds again. The boy's voice had stopped; he stood watching her with that stillness he carried everywhere, as if he had no pulse.

Tears burned at the corners of her eyes, but she bit them back. She wouldn't cry here, not with him, not under the gaze of broken angels. She pressed her sticky hand against her apron, leaving a dark stain that smelled of sweetness already turning sour.

The boy bent, retrieved the fallen apple, and set the broken halves neatly together on the grave. He bowed his head once more, then straightened.

"You heard her," he said. It wasn't a question.

She nodded, throat too tight for words.

They left the graveyard without speaking. The girl's shoes crunched on gravel, louder than she wanted them to be, while the boy moved beside her without sound. The apple's sweetness lingered on her skin.

She rubbed her hand against her apron but the smell clung, faint and insistent, a reminder she couldn't wash away.

The iron gate moaned as it closed behind them. The night opened up again, but it felt thinner now, stretched across something vast and unknowable.

They walked past shuttered houses with lace curtains pulled tight, dogs barking halfheartedly from behind fences. Streetlamps hummed, drawing moths into frantic spirals. She glanced at the boy, his face unreadable in the shifting pools of light and shadow. She wanted to ask what he had done, how he had known, why he had carried an apple into the night as if it were already meant for her. But the words snagged in her throat.

They reached the main road, where traffic lights clicked through their cycle even with no cars waiting. A lone bus roared past, scattering chip wrappers along the gutter. She thought of the voice again — *Every day* — and her chest ached with a grief she didn't know how to name. It wasn't loss, not exactly. It was proof of love too late to change anything. Proof she had been wanted. Proof that absence had not meant indifference.

At the corner, the boy finally spoke. "It's yours now," he said. Three words that landed like a stone in water, ripples spreading outward. She didn't know if he meant the memory, the truth, or something heavier she hadn't yet understood.

She looked at her feet, confused, a question on her lips. When she lifted her head, he was gone. No footsteps, no shadow — only the faint sweetness of clove smoke unspooling into the night. For a heartbeat she wondered if she'd imagined him. And yet, instead of fear, a strange calm settled in her chest, as though he'd left something with her — not a burden, but a spell stitched quiet and unseen.

She paused on the threshold, letting the heat wrap her again, letting the smell of fried food crawl back into her clothes. The lanterns swayed faintly overhead, their colors dulled but still casting soft light. She touched her apron pocket out of habit, fingertips brushing the crushed clove cigarette packet, the faint sweetness of tobacco and spice rising in her mind.

The owner appeared in the kitchen doorway, rag over his shoulder, steam clinging to him like a second skin. He clicked his tongue, waved his hand — *tch tch tch* — and disappeared again. The rhythm of the place resumed, undisturbed.

She stepped back behind the counter and picked up her rag. The tables were still sticky, the floor still pulled at her feet. Still, the steam curled around her like a promise, and for the first time she felt less hollow, as if she could endure the night ahead.

Deadlines and Doughnuts

"You should take the next train out of here," the man beside me said.

His voice startled me because I hadn't noticed him sit down. I looked up and down the platform, but we were the only two people waiting. His words seemed to hang in the cold air, oddly heavy, as though they carried a meaning I wasn't yet privy to.

"Pardon?" I asked, pulling my coat tighter.

"You should take the next train out of here," he repeated, slower this time, as though the words carried more weight than simple advice.

"Well, I intended to...but...er...thanks," I managed. My voice came out thinner than I would have liked, forced into politeness.

He studied me with a look that suggested *I* was the strange one. His dark hair looked as if it hadn't felt the touch of soap or water for days. The long, beige coat he wore sagged heavily around him, creased in unnatural folds and blotched with stains that told the story of spilled food. His stubble was uneven, a half-grown beard that spoke of neglect rather than style.

The longer he looked at me, the more I wanted to shrink away. I shifted in my seat, subtly turning my shoulders, angling my body just enough to place distance between us. My hands busied themselves with nervous gestures—brushing imaginary crumbs from my skirt, smoothing the fabric that didn't need smoothing, patting at my bobbed hair though it lay neatly against my face.

Then his hand—rough, unwashed, nails black at the edges—landed squarely on my shoulder.

My chest seized with panic.

"No, no!" he said quickly, seeing my reaction. His tone was urgent, almost pleading. "It's not what you think. It's a special train. It's coming for you. You should take it."

His words made no sense. My instincts screamed to get away. I stood so abruptly my bag slipped against my hip, and I backed away, step by step.

"Um, sure. I'll take it," I muttered, my voice too bright, too rushed. Anything to appease him. I moved quickly up the platform, breath steaming in the chill air. My laptop bag thumped against my hip as I adjusted the strap higher. I kept my eyes forward, refusing to risk another glance at Mr. Crazy.

Where was my train? It was already five minutes late. No announcements, no explanation. My deadlines ticked at the back of my mind. I needed to get to the office.

That was when the gust came.

A sudden, forceful sweep of air, cold enough to bite through fabric and skin. My breath clouded in front of me, and from nowhere, a train appeared.

I froze.

It hadn't come down the line—hadn't appeared gradually in the distance, growing larger with sound and motion like every other train I had ever seen. No. This one was simply *there*.

And it wasn't my train.

It was a steam engine. Massive. Black. Alive with sound and motion. The whistle screamed, piercing the air, while the chug and hiss of its breathing machinery filled the platform like a giant's heartbeat. The brakes screeched as it ground to a halt, the noise sharp enough to make me flinch. Heat shimmered off its iron sides, rippling the air.

I stared, blinking against the sudden blast of steam. Perhaps there was some historical event today? Some vintage exhibition I hadn't heard about? I'd never seen a train like this here before.

The driver leapt down from the engine. His clothes were streaked with coal dust, his cap tilted back on his head. Planting his hands on his hips, he looked straight at me and shouted, "Well, what are you waiting for? This is your train. Jump on!"

My head whipped around instinctively, searching the platform. But the man in the coat—the one who had spoken to me, warned me—was gone.

"My train?" I asked. "I'm waiting for the seven-thirty-five to the city. Surely this isn't it."

The driver pulled off his cap and scratched his head, leaving a dark smudge across his forehead. "Not sure what you mean, love, but I've no time to wait around. Jump on!" His voice carried the blunt impatience of someone who had schedules I couldn't begin to understand.

I hesitated, torn between logic and curiosity. This train didn't belong here—it couldn't—but its presence was undeniable. Against all better judgment, I stepped forward, edging past the hissing engine, which pulsed like some great living beast.

The carriage I chose was wooden, old-fashioned, polished once but dulled by time. Its windows were streaked with mist, and when I peered inside, I saw nothing: no passengers, no movement, just rows of empty seats.

Still, something compelled me. My hand closed around the cold metal handle, and I pushed the door open.

The moment I stepped inside, the train lurched forward. I lost my balance, stumbling against the wall as it hurtled down the tracks with sudden, furious speed. Faster, faster—the rhythm of the wheels pounding in my chest.

Panic rose. My stomach flipped in protest, and I looked wildly about the carriage, desperate for some sign of control.

That was when I saw him.

The man from the platform.

He was seated calmly now, as if he had always been there. His expression was smug, his smile unsettling. He patted the seat beside him with a kind of theatrical flourish, as though this were a game he'd been waiting for me to play.

"Isaac Salt," he said, offering a hand.

My gaze flicked down to his fingers. Nails blackened, skin rough, a faint trace of dirt caught beneath the creases. I didn't take it.

He let out a small laugh, withdrawing his hand but never breaking eye contact. "And you are?"

I hesitated. My throat felt dry.

"Oh, never mind, Miss," he said, waving away my silence. "I know who you are." His grin widened. "Lucy Quinn."

The sound of my own name startled me more than the train itself. I clutched at my coat, instinctively searching for a tag, a badge, anything I might have forgotten to remove after yesterday's conference. Nothing. No clue as to how he could know me.

"You—how do you know that? What is this? What's happening?" My voice cracked as I gestured around us, at the glossy wood paneling, the brass fittings dulled by age, the entire absurdity of it.

Isaac spread his arms wide as though presenting a grand truth. "It's a train, Miss Quinn." He tilted his head, eyes gleaming. "A train."

"It's not the seven-thirty-five," I said firmly, though my conviction faltered even as I spoke the words.

He pressed a finger to his lips, a conspiratorial hush. His grin danced across his face, refusing to be contained. "No, no. It's a special train. For you, Miss Lucy Quinn."

Hearing my name again on his lips made my skin prickle. I swallowed hard, tucking a strand of hair nervously behind my ear, my mind racing. The sensible part of me screamed not to engage, not to encourage whatever this was, but silence felt more dangerous than speech.

Isaac suddenly pressed his face against the glass, fogging it with his breath. "Here we are! Here we are!" His voice was alight with excitement, like a child on the verge of opening a long-awaited gift.

All I saw outside was white—fog or steam, I couldn't tell. The train screeched, brakes grinding, the sudden halt throwing me forward. My hands flew out in time to catch the back of the seat in front, saving me from a graceless fall onto the wooden floor.

Isaac sprang to his feet, sweeping into a bow with exaggerated flourish. "Allow me," he said, offering his hand again.

I recoiled, the sight of his dirty nails enough to twist my stomach. Pushing myself up without his help, I saw the flicker of disappointment on his face. For an instant, I felt a pang of guilt.

I drew in a breath, steadying myself. My body hummed with adrenaline, my nerves stretched thin as wire. Slowly, cautiously, I walked toward the door.

The hiss of the engine was deafening. Moisture hung in the air, tiny droplets dampening my skin. I peered into the whiteness beyond the carriage, my pulse thrumming.

The fog shifted, thinned. Shapes emerged.

An old-fashioned station revealed itself—quaint, almost picturesque. A little waiting room stood to one side, beside a shop with a painted sign. Iron lacework curled across the support beams, green with age. Above it all, a clock face gleamed, its hands frozen as the bell struck one in the afternoon. The sound echoed with too much authority for such a small place.

The clock was wrong. It had to be.

"Look, I really need to get to work," I was saying, clinging to the last threads of normality, when suddenly there was a shove in the small of my back. I stumbled forward off the carriage and onto the platform, nearly tripping.

I whirled, reaching for the train—needing its solidity, its heat—but my hand caught only mist. The engine, the carriages, the smoke: gone. The platform stretched into emptiness behind me.

"Where are we?" My voice echoed unnaturally.

"Nowhere," Isaac replied with a shrug. "Or everywhere. Depends on the day. I never quite know."

The words made me dizzy. The station around me seemed to tilt, its ironwork arches bending and swaying like reeds in the wind. I steadied myself, blinking hard.

Then came a scent. Sweet. Seductive. It curled through the air, wrapping around me like an invisible hand. Cinnamon. Sugar. Doughnuts warm from the fryer.

My stomach clenched. A calmness washed over me, unearned, unnatural. My mind knew I should be afraid, but my body only wanted more of that scent. The office, my deadlines, the city—they felt far away, almost imagined.

When I blinked again, Isaac was closer. His murky green eyes caught mine, his grin both sly and familiar. In that instant, the grime of his coat, the roughness of his jaw, seemed less important than before. His face was lined, textured, but not without a strange ruggedness.

"You're...sort of handsome," I said, surprising myself. My hand patted his cheek as if my body had acted before my mind. Heat rushed to my face. Why would I say that? Perhaps it was the strangeness of the situation, as though the warm haze of sugar and cinnamon had intoxicated me, setting my thoughts adrift from reason.

My palms were damp. My head floated, untethered. Gravity felt optional. The world swayed and spun, and I wondered if I was falling.

Then I was seated in a red booth, though I had no memory of walking inside the station. The vinyl was cracked, a split seam exposing yellow foam. The sweet smell clung to it, thick and cloying, seeping into my skin with every breath.

A small silver bell rested on the table. Isaac reached for it and rang it sharply. The sound was piercing, almost unbearable, ricocheting in my skull. Beneath it, louder still, came the tick of a clock—endless, pounding, as if each second dropped into my head like a stone.

I pressed my hands against my ears. "Make it stop," I whispered.

"Make what stop?" Isaac asked just as a waiter appeared.

The man might have stepped from an old black-and-white film. His moustache was pencil-thin, his dark hair slicked back to perfection, his jaw carved sharp enough to cut glass. His suit was pressed, his movements neat. His eyes, though—piercing blue, unyielding—were far too sharp, far too real.

A laugh bubbled out of me, high and strange. "You're handsome too," I blurted. My hand clamped over my mouth, horrified. *What was wrong with me?*

My thoughts kept tumbling free, unmoored, as though I'd misplaced the filter between mind and mouth.

The waiter's expression didn't change.

"She wants coffee," Isaac said, nodding toward me. "Don't you, Lucy?"

"Yes. No—wait." The words tangled on my tongue. "Ice-cream soda."

Coffee would have been the sensible choice, the one I always made. But just now I needed something different, something that felt like letting go. The doughnut-scented air demanded sweetness, and for once, I couldn't deny it.

The waiter vanished, returning with a glass set upon a saucer. The soda fizzed and overflowed, froth running in tiny rivers. The sound was unbearable: hissing, crackling, alive. It mingled with the ticking clock until it felt as though my head might split open.

I pressed my palms tighter against my ears. My head swam, heavy and light at once. Whatever this was, it wasn't coffee's clear-eyed steadiness. It was something stranger, coming from here—this room, this place.

"Why is there no music?" I demanded, my voice shrill and shaky.

The waiter raised an eyebrow, clicked his tongue with disapproval, and walked away without answering.

"I'd feel better with some music," I whispered to myself, swaying slightly.

Isaac's grin widened, and he gave a small nod. "Ah, now you're getting it," he said, as if the whole point were to loosen my grip on routine — on what was considered *normal*.

"Would you like to dance?"

I laughed, the sound brittle, like glass. "There's no music."

"There will be," he said, taking my hand. His skin was coarse, but I didn't pull away. "The music begins when the dancing does."

My legs moved clumsily, my body swaying without my permission. I felt spellbound. I knew I wasn't. The realization chilled me—the place itself was working on me, bending me to its rhythm, casting a spell with nothing more than its presence.

Out of the corner of my eye, the waiter scowled, his foot tapping hard against the floor, as if keeping time on behalf of the clock. His glare was sharp enough to cut.

"Stop it!" he barked, storming toward us. "There hasn't been music here for years. Order is better than chaos!"

I wanted to snap back, to tell him that a little music, a little fun, was what made all the order bearable. But the thought caught in my throat. Wasn't I the same? Always choosing work over whim, deadlines over doughnuts? The recognition stung.

But Isaac pulled me closer, his breath warm against my cheek.

And then—

The ticking stopped.

Silence fell.

And from that silence, music rose.

It burst into being as though the world itself had been holding its breath. A woman in a long red gown stood at a pedestal microphone, her voice lush and velvety. Beside her, a man played the piano, its polished surface gleaming as though it had never known dust.

The café transformed around us. The air shimmered, alive. Tables seemed brighter, fresher, as though scrubbed clean by the sound itself.

The waiter shouted, furious, trying to wrench me away. "Enough! Enough!" His voice cracked with desperation. "The music has no place here!"

For a heartbeat, I wanted to agree with him — wasn't I always the one insisting there was no time for indulgence, no room for joy? The thought stung.

But I clung tighter to Isaac. My body swayed freely now, the giddiness flooding me with joy. A laugh bubbled out of me, reckless and unstoppable. "The music feels wonderful!" I cried. And it did. It felt like freedom.

I don't remember when the music stopped, or when the piano faded, or when the singer in red slipped back into silence. One moment I was laughing in Isaac's arms, the next I was blinking into mist.

The cold bit at me. My breath came out in clouds. I was no longer in the café, no longer on the dance floor—I was back on the same platform where it had all begun.

The familiar bench was beneath me. My phone glowed in my hand: 7:30. Five minutes until the next train.

Had I dreamt it? The train, the station, Isaac, the music?

I touched my cheek, still warm, as if from someone's hand. My hair was mussed, strands falling free from the neat bob I'd smoothed that morning. A pang of disappointment swept through me, sharp and heavy. I hadn't realized how tightly I had been holding on to myself until the dance had pried me loose.

For a moment, I sat frozen, unwilling to believe it was gone.

Then I heard it.

Faint, but unmistakable. The whistle of a steam train. The sound carried across the tracks like a secret only I was meant to hear. My heart leapt.

I turned to the woman beside me—a woman I hadn't noticed sitting there before. She was composed, immaculate, her red lipstick sharp against pale skin. "Can you hear it?" I asked. "The steam train whistle?"

She tilted her head, listening. "Yes…I think I can. That's odd, isn't it?"

Odd. That word seemed too small. I smiled but said nothing, rising from the bench. My legs felt lighter than they had in years.

Deadlines would still be waiting. My inbox would still be filling. My hair would never stay perfectly in place. But for the first time, none of that seemed to matter quite as much. There was more to life than neat lines and polished surfaces. There was music, and dancing, and the wild, reckless joy of letting go.

A laugh escaped me, sudden and irrepressible, bubbling up from somewhere new. I walked down the platform, my step lighter, freer.

And there he was.

The man in the beige coat leaned against the wall, a folded newspaper in his hands. At our first meeting I'd thought him rumpled, even a little lost, like someone who didn't belong. But now the looseness in his collar, the untamed hair falling across his forehead, looked less like neglect and more like freedom. He wasn't polished, not precise — and maybe that was the point. Neat and orderly didn't always matter.

He looked up as though he had been expecting me, a knowing smile tugging at his lips.

"Isaac," I whispered.

His eyes caught mine, gleaming with mischief. He winked.

A Garden Between Seasons

She lay flat on the kitchen floor, the tiles cold and unyielding beneath her back. It felt safe here. She pressed her palms against them—bleach clung to the grout, stinging her nose, while the heavier scent of dirt lingered in the corners her scrubbing had missed.

On this August night in Salem, voices rose in a low hum—laughter climbing the narrow streets. From her kitchen floor, Amber listened, feeling lonelier with every shout of joy that floated past her window.

She closed her eyes. The laughter outside belonged to people who had roots here—friends spilling out of restaurants, families lingering on the sidewalks, voices rising and falling in easy harmony. She imagined them all belonging to each other, while she belonged to no one.

A sigh left her chest and sank into the floor. Loneliness, sharp and heavy, pulled at her stomach. She sat up abruptly, refusing to let the feeling swallow her whole. What was the point of coming to a new place only to spend eternity inside, lying on a kitchen floor like some forgotten rag?

Amber pushed herself up, brushed the dust from her jeans, and grabbed her purse. She refused to hide. Not tonight. She needed the press of people around her, even if she never spoke a word to them.

The wooden stairs leading from her apartment groaned beneath her steps, each one wobbling faintly as though testing her resolve. She ran her hand along the railing, the paint peeling in brittle curls that flaked beneath her fingers.

Outside, the evening air held the day's leftover heat, but a breeze was beginning to slip through the streets. She walked with her head held high, determined to look as though she belonged, even as her stomach turned in knots. Just breath, she told herself.

Charter Street stretched ahead, dotted with people laughing and talking, couples leaning close, families tugging children along. Amber passed them all, her stride brisk, her face carefully arranged into calm indifference.

The good thing about this time of year, she thought, was that there weren't as many tourists. By autumn, the streets would be packed with Halloween crowds—a carnival of chaos, for better and worse. Business owners would thrive, but the city itself would suffer. Tonight, though, the streets breathed a little easier.

Still, the clusters of sightseers were impossible to avoid. She passed a group gathered outside the old graveyard, their guide gesturing animatedly while the tourists clutched brochures and phones. Amber quickened her pace.

She reached Essex Street, where shopfronts gleamed with glass displays of crystals, spell books, and witchcraft paraphernalia. Normally, she admired them. Normally, she would pause to study the charms and posters, soaking in the promise of mystery. Tonight, though, she kept moving, her whole body humming with restless anxiety.

At the corner she paused before a building tied to Salem's darkest hours. The original meetinghouse was long gone, yet the memories still clung to this place, where accusations had once been spoken in tones as solemn as sermons.

Centuries ago, children and teenagers fed whispers of suspicion until fear twisted into power, condemning hundreds of innocents as witches. Even now, the town seemed to hum with judgment. Amber shivered and looked away. onight wasn't about those long-ago witches—it was about her story, a story she hadn't yet found the words for.

She turned onto Chestnut Street. The homes here were palatial—remnants of wealth, sprawling mansions from another century, their grand facades still intact. Gas lamps flickered on either side of the street, their glow softened by the shade of towering oaks. She felt herself slowing. The whisper of leaves followed the breeze, gentle, almost protective, and for the first time that Summer evening, she felt herself begin to breathe more evenly.

A small bird chirped overhead. Amber tilted her face to the branches, spotting two little shapes flitting about a larger one. A mother and her chicks, she thought, watching as they darted between leaves. Their world was self-contained, safe, whole.

On her right, a black iron gate stood open. Its hinges sagged, one nearly torn from the stone post. Beyond it stretched a garden, perhaps once the manicured lawn of a mansion, now surrendered to the public. The grass was overgrown, and shadows reached long across its edges, but the sight of the open space tugged at her.

Amber slipped through the gate. The metal groaned faintly under her hand, the sound quickly lost in the rustle of the trees. A stone bench waited just inside. She crossed to it and eased herself onto the seat, her body thankful for the pause.

The breeze picked up, tugging at her hair, pushing cold fingers across her arms. She rubbed them briskly, wishing she'd thought to bring a jacket.

Closing her eyes, she allowed her body to grow still. For a moment she imagined she could hear the ocean. Of course, she knew it was miles away, yet the sound rose and fell in her ears as if carried inland on the wind. Another fragrance threaded through the air, sweet and faintly floral, though she couldn't place its source. She breathed deeply, letting it fill her chest.

Above her, the little birds were still playing, their wings beating soft against the branches. For a while, she forgot she was lonely.

Children's laughter drifted through the air. At first faint, then louder, then faint again, rising and falling like waves against the shore.

Amber sat straighter on the bench, her eyes opening slowly. The garden was empty. Still, the sound curled around her, tugging at her senses.

The laughter stopped abruptly. In its place came a pressure in the air, subtle but undeniable, like a shift in atmosphere before a storm. The skin prickled at the back of her neck. A tingling sensation trickling from her scalp down the length of her spine.

Someone was here. She felt it as surely as she felt the stone beneath her.

Amber forced herself to breathe evenly. She didn't want to open her eyes, didn't want to see what she inctively knew was standing too close—but she had already opened them. The garden remained empty. The shadows of the trees swayed. Nothing else.

She rolled her shoulders, shook out her hands as if to fling away the tension.

And then the laughter came again, closer this time.

Amber jumped.

A girl in a white dress spun in circles just a few feet away, her small arms lifted as though she were dancing with the wind. Her voice pealed high and bright, the sound of pure joy. A boy stood beside her, watching with calm eyes. He looked about the same age, perhaps her brother, his suspenders tugged over a simple shirt, a cap shadowing his face.

They looked like children from a vintage photograph.

Amber blinked, unsure. A wedding party, she thought wildly. A period costume event. Some sort of reenactment. That had to be it. It was too early for Halloween.

The girl stopped mid-spin. Her eyes widened when they landed on Amber. Her mouth opened slightly.

"Hello," the girl said. Her voice was clear as a bell. "Are you a fairy?"

Amber let out a nervous laugh. "Maybe," she said, the word half a joke, half an attempt to hide her unease.

The boy tilted his head, studying her with an expression too serious for his age.

The girl took one hesitant step forward, then stopped again. "Your clothes are strange."

Amber glanced down at herself. Black jeans. A plain t-shirt. Nothing unusual. It was *their* clothes that were strange.

"Are you going to a wedding?" Amber asked, searching for logic, for something to explain them.

The children exchanged a look, their brows furrowed in silent question.

Far in the distance, a bell tolled the hour. The sound rang too deep, too resonant, filling the garden like a command.

The last of the twilight seemed to falter. The light thinned, as if drawn away, while clouds gathered fast and low, thickening the sky to gray. A sharp wind rose, rushing through the branches and bending them hard until the birds scattered into silence.

Amber rubbed her arms, cold seeping into her skin. She turned sharply toward the children.

They were gone.

Her breath caught. She hadn't heard them leave. Not a single footstep. Were they ghosts, lingering spirits? The thought shivered through her, and she faltered, wondering why she feared them. If they were still here, didn't that mean she wasn't entirely alone?

The tingling sensation returned, stronger, flooding her spine. A presence hovered at her shoulder, unseen but pressing. She gasped and spun, but the garden was empty again.

Panic nipped at her throat. She bolted from the bench and hurried toward the gate.

The iron gate loomed before her, no longer sagging on one hinge. The metal stood firm, straight, as though it had never known rust. She didn't stop to wonder how.

She stumbled out onto Chestnut Street. At first glance it was unchanged: the row of grand houses still stood in silence, their trees whispering above. But the lamps at their gates no longer glowed with steady electric light. Instead, candleflame flickered faintly through curtained windows, leaving the street in long stretches of shadow.

For an instant, Amber thought she saw one lit by a steady yellow bulb, warm and modern, the kind she passed every night. But when she blinked, only wavering flame remained.

Her heart hammered. She turned and ran, feet striking hard against the stones, desperate for the familiarity of Essex Street.

When she reached the crossroads at Washington, she stopped dead.

The enclosed pedestrian mall was gone. In its place, horse-drawn streetcars rumbled along metal tracks, wheels screeching faintly as hooves clattered against the cobblestones. The air was sharp with the smell of manure, the tang of iron, the sourness of stale beer.

Beneath it all, just for a breath, she caught another smell — acrid and chemical, like exhaust. A hiss rose at her back, so like the sigh of a bus brake that she turned, certain she'd find one behind her. Only horses clattered past.

Amber blinked hard, her pulse racing. Women in long dresses hurried past, their skirts brushing her arms. Men in bowler hats puffed at pipes, casting her sidelong looks as though she were some offense to their order.

Her skin turned cold. Blood drained from her face.

This couldn't be real. It couldn't.

But the headache blooming at her temples told her otherwise.

A sharp tug at her sleeve made Amber flinch.

She looked down. A barefoot boy, his face smeared with dirt, grinned up at her with crooked teeth. His eyes glinted with mischief as if he'd been waiting for her all along.

Amber recoiled.

Before she could pull back, another hand slipped gently into hers. Small. Familiar.

Relief surged through her when she saw the girl in white. She looked exactly as she had in the garden, only sharper now, more vivid in the lamplight, as though she belonged fully to this place.

"Oh, it's you," Amber whispered, half-shaky, half-relieved. "You disappeared from the garden."

The girl tilted her head, her expression puzzled. "We can't stay there all the time," she said softly, as if explaining something obvious. "Not everyone makes it through. But I knew you would." Her smile widened, quick and bright. "I knew you weren't a fairy."

The barefoot boy scowled, and slunk away toward the gutter, where other children were tossing pebbles in the dust.

The girl squeezed Amber's hand, steady and sure. "Come with me," she said simply, as though the command required no explanation. Amber hesitated, glancing around. "Wait — where's your brother? The boy who was with you in the garden?"

The girl's smile faltered. For a moment her eyes looked older than her face. "Not everyone makes it through," she said again, softer this time. "Sometimes the garden keeps them."

She tugged Amber across Washington Street, weaving between the horses and carts with surprising ease.

Amber stumbled to keep up. Her senses were assaulted at once: the acrid reek of horse manure, the rank stench of urine soaking into the cobblestones, the sourness of spilled beer drifting from a nearby tavern. Her throat tightened, and she gagged, covering her nose with her free hand.

Shops lined the street, but none of them sold crystals or candles. No signs promising tarot readings or psychic consultations. Instead, wooden façades leaned over narrow doorways. A cooper's workshop smelled of tar and sawdust. A tailor's window displayed bolts of wool. She blinked, trying to reconcile this vision with the street she had walked only an hour before.

On her left, a bar loomed crooked, as if the weight of too many patrons had pushed its walls outward. Men in rough coats spilled through the doorway, laughing and swearing, their words slurred by ale. Their cheeks were ruddy, their collars stained. When they spotted her, a few called out, their voices thick with mockery.

Amber froze. Heat flooded her face. She gripped the little girl's hand tighter.

The girl sighed, as though used to this sort of attention. "Come," she said again, tugging Amber toward a side alley.

They darted into its narrow shadow.

From the darkness of a brick wall came the sound of a hacking cough. Amber's steps faltered.

A woman emerged from the shadows. Her hat was held thin, sad feathers and sagged with age and filth. Her dress was frayed, her shawl torn. Her nose was nearly gone, her skin pocked and pale, her eyes unfocused. She dragged a hand across her face, leaving a smear of grime.

For a heartbeat, neon light shimmered faintly on the wall behind her — the hazy violet glow of a psychic's sign Amber knew from modern Essex Street. She blinked and it was gone.

"Spare a coin, miss?" the woman rasped, her voice cracked and raw.

Amber shuddered, her stomach twisting. It felt as if the woman's clouded eyes pierced straight through her, seeing more than her flesh.

The girl tugged her hand sharply. "Don't look. Keep walking."

Amber obeyed. She let herself be pulled further down the alley, her pulse hammering in her ears.

As they broke into the light of an open street, Amber tore her hand away. "I can't do this," she gasped. "I don't know this place. I don't know why I'm here. I just want to go home—back through the garden."

The girl stopped, tilting her head. "The garden?"

"Yes." Amber nodded quickly. "The one with the stone bench and the big oak tree. I came from there. Something happened—I don't know what, but I think it started there. Maybe it can take me back."

The girl's brow furrowed. "You mean our garden?"

Amber blinked. "Yours?"

The girl nodded slowly. "My home."

Frustration twisted in Amber's chest; the girl's vagueness made no sense. Every word felt like smoke, slipping through her grasp. "I just want to go home," Amber whispered. "Back to my time. Back to where I came from."

The girl studied her for a long moment, her eyes wide and solemn. Then she said softly, "If you can find your way from our garden, maybe it will let you go home."

The girl took Amber's hand once more, her fingers cool and steady, and led her back through the twisting streets.

Amber's mind whirled. Every corner, every face, every smell pressed against her until it felt as though her skin might split from the weight of it all. She wanted to run, to scream, to deny all of it—but the girl's hand anchored her, guiding her forward.

And then, at last, Amber recognized the wide sweep of Chestnut Street. The mansions rose on either side like silent witnesses, their windows catching the faint light. Relief stirred in her chest. She was close.

"There," she whispered, spotting the black iron fence. Its gate stood open again, beckoning her. Darkness pooled beyond, but she would take that over the stares of strangers and the filth of streets that weren't hers.

The girl slowed as they reached the threshold. Candlelight flickered from the house next door, shadows shifting against the glass. The birds had gone silent in the darkness.

Amber pulled free, stumbling into the garden. Her legs gave out, and she fell to her knees in the damp grass. The chill seeped through her jeans, grounding her.

Her breath came fast and shallow. Her heart beat wildly, as though trying to escape her chest.

She dropped onto her back, staring up at the branches above. The cool blades of grass threaded between her fingers, sharp and wet. She clung to them like lifelines.

When she opened her eyes again, the little girl was still there, hovering above her. Her face was curious, her white dress glowing faintly in the dimness.

Amber blinked once. The girl blurred. She blinked again, and the features began to dissolve, fading like smoke in the air.

The girl's lips moved. Words tumbled out, but Amber couldn't catch them. A murmur, distant and distorted, like a voice underwater.

"Wait," Amber whispered, her hand lifting toward her. "Please—"

The girl's outline wavered. Her eyes lingered a moment longer, wide and solemn, and then she was gone.

The garden was empty.

Amber lay still, her hand suspended in the air where the girl had been. The garden seemed empty — but the longer she listened, the more she realized it wasn't.

THistory wasn't only trials and verdicts. It breathed in the lives that never reached the books—the delighted spin of a child, boys darting through crooked streets, the drunken spill of laughter into gutters, the rasp of a woman's cough in the dark. The air was alive with echoes, not rehearsed tales for tourists but something raw, near, unshakably human.

They lingered here, their spirits stitched into stone and shadow, close enough to walk beside her. She could feel them brushing against her, urging her to see that she wasn't alone. But fear rose like a wall, turning their presence into unease instead of comfort.

And still, beneath it all, the girl's hand remained—a warmth not of flesh but of spirit, a tether that hadn't faded. Protection, yes, but also an invitation. If she could loosen her grip on fear, perhaps she could feel the truth of it: that the dead did not leave, that they could guide her, even here.

Everyone spoke of Salem as if it belonged only to the trials, as if history could be reduced to ropes and names on a list. But that was only one story. Beneath it, around it, inside it, lived countless more. Forgotten lives. Watching lives. And now she could sense them waiting.

The thought steadied her. Salem wasn't hollow. It was crowded, layered, alive. She closed her eyes and let their presence move through her. Maybe she had never been as alone as she thought—only too afraid to notice.

The Transit Room

She woke with the taste of sleep still thick in her mouth, disoriented by the hush of the room. For a moment she thought she'd overslept—missed her flight, missed everything—but her phone, glowing dimly in her palm, told her she had been gone less than an hour.

Tamsin sighed. Two more hours until her flight. Two more until she was in the air, heading home and her daughter waiting there. The thought tugged at her chest.

Two months apart had felt like forever, and the absence only sharpened the guilt she'd carried all year. Work, travel, excuses—one way or another, she hadn't been around. Now her daughter was a teenager, old enough to need her mother in a different way, and Tamsin felt like a bad mother due to her absence.

She closed her eyes for a moment, picturing her daughter's face, promising herself she'd hold her a little tighter this time.

The strip of light beneath the door pulsed a soft amber, nothing like the sterile glare she remembered when she first lay down. It reminded her of dusk falling through autumn leaves, warm and inviting.

She hesitated, bare feet against the laminate floor, and reached for the handle.

The door swung open on silence.

The corridor beyond was not the narrow, whitewashed passage she'd walked earlier but something older: planks of wood underfoot, walls paneled in dark timber, lanterns hung at intervals casting their honeyed glow. The air smelled of smoke and rain-soaked earth, as if she'd stepped into a memory of some country inn she had never visited.

No voices. No wheels dragging across tile. No distant echo of boarding calls.

Tamsin shook her head. Probably the pill, she thought. Zolpidem. She'd read the articles—sleepwalkers cooking whole meals in their kitchens, driving cars they didn't remember starting. She should never have taken it on a layover, but exhaustion and lack of sleep had made the choice for her.

Even so, her grandmother's voice flickered across her mind as she stared down the empty hall—half-forgotten stories about inns at crossroads, about travelers who took the wrong turn and found themselves somewhere unexpected. She shook her head hard, banishing the thought. She was jetlagged, not cursed.

Tamsin closed the door and lay back down, turning her face to the wall. But the glow seeped in regardless, pooling on the floor, an amber stain she couldn't ignore.

Finally, with a sigh, she swung her legs over the side of the bed. She slipped the keycard from the desk into her palm as though it were a talisman.

The handle was cool beneath her fingers.

Tamsin stepped into the corridor.

She turned back, half-expecting the room to be gone, but the doorway still framed the sleek capsule she'd entered only hours ago.

The air felt different here—damp, carrying the faint tang of woodsmoke and something older, something like wet leaves. Her bare feet should have met carpet, the flat scratch of synthetic weave, but the floor beneath her was uneven, ridged like timber worn smooth by years of passing boots.

She froze, glanced back. The doorway was still there, a neat white rectangle, her suitcase propped in the corner just as she'd left it. A blink, a step forward, and maybe it would all snap back to normal.

She touched the wall. Not painted plasterboard but dark wood, cool under her fingertips.

"This isn't real," she whispered. Her voice sounded small in the silence.

She moved a little further, the keycard clutched tight in her fist. The corridor stretched ahead, lanterns casting pools of amber light. They flickered faintly, not with electricity but with flame.

Her stomach lurched. She hadn't seen a lantern like that since childhood, in her grandmother's house—the one where the power cut out every winter storm and her gran would light a stubby candle. Those stories about magical crossroads started to feel less like fiction. Tamsin shook her head again, dismissing it as the effects of the Zolpide but the thought of Cornish piskies stayed strong in her mind. Mischievous creatures that thrived on leading wanderers astray. A glimmer of light on the moors, a voice calling your name when no one was there—follow it, and you'd lose your way entirely.

Those were children's tales, nothing more. Yet the hush of the hall pressed close, as if waiting, and the old warnings would not be banished.

A sharp crack split the silence.

She spun around just as the door to her hotel room slammed shut with a heavy bang. The sound reverberated down the corridor, sharp and final, like a gavel.

Her pulse kicked. She rushed back, fumbling the keycard in her hand.

But the doorway was gone. No sleek capsule, no strip of sterile light, no suitcase in the corner. Only a seamless wall of dark wood from floor to ceiling, the lantern glow painting it gold.

Tamsin pressed her palm flat against it, breath ragged. Nothing yielded. It was as though the room had never been there at all.

She stood with her hand against the wall until the cold bit into her skin. Slowly, she lowered it, the keycard still clutched uselessly in her fist.

The corridor stretched in both directions, long and hollow, the lanterns marking out pools of light like islands in the dark. Beyond each glow was shadow, dense and silent, waiting.

Her breathing was too loud. Each exhale seemed to echo back at her, as though the hall were imitating her in some quiet game. She took a step forward and the floorboards groaned beneath her, the sound swallowed almost instantly by the hush.

There was no murmur of televisions through thin walls, no doors slamming, no distant laughter. None of the anonymous noises she expected in any hotel. Only silence. A silence so complete it pressed against her eardrums until she wondered if she'd gone deaf.

Her mouth was dry. She licked her lips, testing the word that rose without thought: *Hello?*

But she swallowed it down again. Instinct told her not to break the stillness, as if words would confirm the strangeness of this place, make it real.

Tamsin walked, the hush pressing tighter with every step. The corridor narrowed, the lanterns thinning until whole stretches lay in shadow, the glow ahead her only anchor.

Doors lined the hall, each one identical, brass handles gleaming faintly in the dim light. She tried one at random, then another. Locked. So was the next.

She kept going.

At first she thought the passage ended in darkness, but as her eyes adjusted, she saw it: a door standing alone at the far end. Older than the rest, its wood looked rough-hewn, scarred by age, the grain dark as if it had drunk in centuries.

She slowed.

A faint light leaked through the cracks, not the sharp white of bulbs, not the flicker of flame. It pulsed slow and steady, as though it had a heartbeat.

The corridor stretched like an arrow pointing her on.

Her grandmother's tales rose again, unbidden—piskies luring the unwary from the safe path, crossroads that offered not shelter but choice – and not necessarily a good choice. Don't follow strange lights, her gran had warned, don't trust the glow where none should be.

Yet her feet carried her forward.

The closer she came, the stronger the sense of recognition, like déjà vu threading her chest. The smell of woodsmoke, faint and sweet. A whisper of voices just beyond the wood, blurred and half-heard, though she couldn't make out a single word.

She stopped before the door, her breath catching.

The glow shivered once, as if acknowledging her.

It was obvious she was meant to go inside.

Tamsin pressed the keycard tighter in her palm, though she knew it was useless here. The handle was warm beneath her hand, faintly throbbing, as if something on the other side was alive and waiting.

She drew a breath and turned it.

The door swung inward without a sound.

Warmth spilled over her—smoke, peat, the low orange glow of fire. She blinked, certain her eyes were playing tricks. This wasn't a hotel room. The air was thick with the scent of wood ash and herbs hanging from a beam overhead. A table squatted in the center, scarred and stained, rushes scattered across the floor.

For a moment she hovered on the threshold, waiting for the vision to tear like paper, for carpet and plaster to return. But nothing shifted. The place was solid, lived in.

Her gaze caught on the small details: a wooden spoon left beside a clay bowl, as though someone had only just set it down. A shawl draped over a chair, the wool still holding the shape of shoulders. A child's toy—carved roughly from wood—abandoned near the hearth.

A shiver crawled down her spine. None of this belonged to her. And yet... her hand itched to pick up the spoon, to test its weight. The shawl looked familiar, though she couldn't say why. Even the toy tugged at her, stirring a tenderness so sharp it made her throat ache.

Her pulse raced. Zolpidem couldn't conjure this. Dream or not, she felt the truth of it in her bones.

A gust stirred the rushes on the floor, carrying with it the faint echo of laughter—soft, fleeting, a sound she almost knew.

Tamsin stepped inside.

She moved carefully, each step sinking into the rushes with a faint crackle. The warmth of the fire wrapped around her, the light painting the walls in restless gold.

Her fingers brushed the back of the chair where the shawl hung. The wool was coarse, worn thin at the edges, but when she lifted it, the scent rose up—smoke and heather and something almost like her own skin. The familiarity was so sharp she pressed the fabric to her face before she could stop herself.

Her eyes stung.

On the table, the clay bowl still held the dregs of stew, a slick of fat cooling on the surface. She picked up the spoon beside it. Its handle was smoothed by years of use, the curve fitting her palm as though it belonged there. She ran her thumb along the groove her hand had known before.

The fire popped. She turned sharply, half-expecting someone to be there—a man shrugging off his coat, a child crouched by the hearth. For a moment, she saw it: a coat slung over the peg by the door, a small figure bending to set a log on the flames. The image flickered like breath on glass and was gone.

Her heart lurched. She gripped the spoon tighter, as if it were proof that what she saw was more than a dream.

A laugh rose in the air then, clearer this time. High, sweet, tumbling with the delight of a child. It filled her chest with an ache so deep it was almost joy, almost grief.

She turned toward the sound, her throat tight.

By the hearth, a small figure shifted into view. A child crouched low, balancing a log in both hands, the firelight gilding hair that shone like copper. The laugh bubbled again as the log tipped, scattering sparks that leapt up the chimney.

Tamsin's breath caught. She knew that laugh, that tumble of joy that lived somewhere behind her ribs. It wasn't her daughter's laugh, not exactly, but it echoed in the same place. Something in her recognized it with the force of memory, as if she had once loved this child too—loved and lost.

The figure turned slightly, half in shadow, half in flame, and the outline of a cheek, a nose, a mouth soft with youth came into focus. For a dizzying instant she was certain she would know the exact shade of those eyes if they met hers.

Her lips again tried to shape a name. Not a name she'd ever spoken, not one she'd read, but a name that fell into her like a stone dropped into water. A name she had once whispered in another life.

The child stilled. The log slipped from their hands and rolled to the side with a dull thud. Slowly, the head lifted, as if they had heard her.

Their gaze began to turn toward her—

And the fire shuddered, the walls trembling with it. The rushes scattered, the room blurred at the edges like wet ink.

"No—" The word tore out of her as she reached forward, the spoon clattering from her hand.

But the vision was breaking, unravelling into shadow and silence.

She fell, landing hard on her knees against the boards of the corridor. The spoon was gone. The shawl. The fire. Only the hush remained, pressing in close.

The glowing door no longer pulsed. In its place stood the clean, sterile hallway of the airport hotel. The strip of light shone white again from beneath her door, harsh and ordinary.

Her hand shook as she swiped the keycard. This time, it worked. The door unlocked with a mechanical click, swinging back to reveal her suitcase waiting neatly in the corner, the bed smooth and impersonal.

She stood in the doorway for a long moment, staring at the familiar room. The air was flat with disinfectant, but in her throat still clung the tang of smoke, and in her ears, the phantom trace of a laugh that wasn't hers to keep.

Tamsin pressed the door shut and leaned her forehead against it, eyes stinging. She couldn't name what she had lost, couldn't prove it had ever been real. Only the ache remained, sharp and undeniable, as if her body remembered more than her mind could carry.

She crawled back into bed. The mattress received her like it had never let her go. She lay awake, staring at the ceiling, her chest tight with the weight of what she had seen—or imagined. The glow was gone, the hush broken, but the longing clung to her all the same.

Sleep claimed her anyway.

When her alarm buzzed, she rose automatically, her body remembering the motions: shower, bag zipped, passport checked. The corridor outside was bland, carpeted, empty. Ordinary.

Hours later, as the plane lifted into the morning sky, her thoughts turned again to her daughter. Two weeks apart had felt like forever, but it wasn't only these past weeks that pricked her. It was the long months before them—late nights, excuses, the way she had let the busyness of life steal time she couldn't get back. Her daughter was growing into someone new each day, someone who still needed her, and Tamsin hadn't been there.

She longed for the moment she would hold her again, breathe her in, memorize her face.

And in the marrow of her bones, she understood why that longing cut so deep. Because somewhere, in some life long before this one, she had lost her child. And this time, she would not let go.

Smoke and Rosemary

Elena measured her life by Damien's habits.

The chipped coffee mug abandonedsjaldkfh on the windowsill, always half-drunk and ringed with a faint brown lip she wiped, then wiped again, as if a second pass might clear what the first could not. Shirts in a heap that smelled of cologne and damp pavement—his scent reminded her of deceit. The way his phone never lay face-up, as if even in sleep it might betray him.

Love, she told herself, was supposed to bend. And so she bent, folding around Damien like ivy on crumbling stone, until she no longer knew if the shape in the mirror was hers or just some weird reflection of him. She would catch her likeness in the medicine cabinet and think, briefly, *Who invited you?* Then she would close the cabinet and the room would right itself: toothbrushes paired like quotation marks, the razor with its single sorry hair clinging to the edge, the ache in her shoulders as persistent as a clock.

Damien could charm silence itself. His laughter rang a little too loud, yet people leaned toward it as though it were warmth. He told stories with gestures that crowded the air, made strangers feel drafted into a tale that made them interesting by proximity. He kissed her forehead when she doubted—a priestly, benevolent gesture—and she mistook that for tenderness. But lately the air shifted around him. Lightbulbs flickered overhead like nervous eyelids. A glass cracked in her hand once while she was washing it, a hairline fracture hissing itself into being across the surface like ice. Her cat, Osiris—Ozzy, when they were on speaking terms—stared into the corners of the living room and hissed softly, a white noise of disapproval.

She told herself it was just stress. She'd trained her mind to look for patterns, and now she was finding whole constellations in grains of salt. She'd read that our brains crave stories, and it felt unfair to be wired to make sense of things but then blamed for reading too much into them.

The first slip came on a Thursday. Damien's jacket smelled of smoke, though he didn't smoke. "A bonfire," he said, too quickly. "Friends." He kissed her hair and went to shower. The bathroom door shut and locked with a click. Who has a bonfire and why wasn't she invited?

The next morning, she went to pick the jacket up from where he'd thrown it carelessly in a corner—and a receipt slipped from the inner pocket. A bar she'd never heard of, two glasses of red wine, the total scrawled with a flourish of ink that wasn't his. The server's name signed at the bottom: *Julian.*

She placed it on the counter like evidence and made eggs she didn't want. By the time Damien came out, the receipt had curled at one edge as though trying to roll itself shut.

That night she dreamed of a man lighting candles in a dark room, smoke curling toward the ceiling in words she couldn't read. When she woke, her hair smelled faintly of sage though her apartment held none. She shook her head as if she could rattle sense back into place.

Elena worked in an estoteric bookstore with more windows than customers. It suited her to recommend novels to the three people a day who asked for something that would "fix" them. She would tip her head and say, "All the cures are stacked by the counter," and if they smiled, she liked them. On slow afternoons she shelved books, trying not to think about smoke, bonfires, or how Damien's stories were starting to sound rehearsed.

Two weeks later, rain chased her into a bar she hadn't meant to find. She had been on her way to meet a colleague at a café with real scones, but the sky had performed a sort of sudden confession, opening without warning and delivering sheets that blurred street and glass. She ducked under the first awning, pushed through a heavy door, and stood in the low amber light catching her breath. The bar smelled of wet coats and citrus. At the far end, a bartender peeled an orange with slow precision, coils of rind sliding onto the counter.

A man sat at a table with a book open before him though his eyes weren't on the page. He looked up and met her eyes, as if he'd been expecting her. His smile wasn't flirtatious but knowing, like a shared password between strangers.

"Looks like the sky sent you," he said.

"Elena," she answered even without knowing why, and then felt foolish.

"Julian," he said, which made something in her shoulder unclench—not relief so much as the satisfaction of a puzzle piece finding its place.

The name rattled through her like a pebble down a well. The receipt. The scrawl. Surely, just a coincidence. She glanced at his book. No title on the spine, only a faint embossing that she couldn't make out.

"Is that good?" she asked, because small talk can be the most merciful of spells.

"Just a notebook really," he said, and closed it as if to spare her the sight. He struck a match to light a tealight candle at his table, and for a beat the smoke seemed to braid upon itself, a plaited ribbon that undid into air. She told herself it was a trick of drafts. Then she realized there was no draft.

They spoke of weather and books. His voice flowed like silk drawn across skin, quiet but undeniable. He listened with the attention of someone who had learned precisely how dangerous inattention could be. She noticed his hands—clean, long-fingered, the nails painted black, with a faint crescent of ink near the cuticle of his thumb.

They met again two days later. She told herself it was only convenience—the bar was near her bus stop, the rain kept her there. But it wasn't just convenience anymore when she let a bus go by on purpose. And it wasn't an accident when he said, "I saved this seat for you," and she sat down without pointing out that saving a seat comes with strings attached.

They spoke first of ordinary things, safe distractions that skimmed the surface. Then, in a lull, Elena muttered, "It's exhausting," and realized it was the first honest thing she'd said in days.

The weight she carried had hovered between them since their first meeting, circling like a storm cloud that refused to break. At last it slipped out in fragments—complaints of being unseen, of waiting, of living beside a man whose presence devoured hers. She never spoke his name, as though to name him would conjure him.

Julian didn't prod. He only narrowed his eyes, then nodded once, slow, as if to say *I understand.* It gave her permission. She let the words spill, small disclosures at first, then heavier ones.

He listened as though each syllable were a coin he turned over in his palm. No questions and no diagnosis offered. She enjoyed his company. Most of all, he didn't ask her to explain the man she spoke of. She liked him for that so fiercely it frightened her.

It was on their third meeting that the name broke water, casual, almost careless.

"Damien's late again," Julian muttered, glancing at his phone. "Always late. You'd think after months he'd—"

He stopped when he saw her go still, her face drained of its usual composure.

Elena felt something click at the base of her skull, sharp as a lock turning. "Damien?" she asked. The question left her lips like a garment that no longer fit, sagging from the shoulders, impossible to wear again.

Julian looked up. "Yes. Damien. My... whatever he is." He tried for a smile, but it landed nowhere, belonging to no emotion she could name. He set his phone face-down. The candle on the table guttered once, then steadied itself as though nothing had happened.

For a moment neither spoke. They both just knew they were talking about the same man. Around them, the bar carried on, other conversations swelling and falling like waves that would never touch their shore.

Julian was first. He tapped his knuckle lightly against the table. "Well," he said at last. "That explains a lot."

Elena pressed her palms hard against the wood to stop herself from picking at the varnish. The old training in her spine returned—the lesson of not making a scene, of keeping her voice pitched to the octave of acceptable. She was struck by the sudden urge to straighten the candles between them, to make them symmetrical. Just as quickly, she felt an almost violent need to leave them crooked.

They might have walked away from each other but instead Julian raised his glass. "To surviving Damien," he said, and managed to put kindness in the sentence.

She touched hers to his. "To surviving." The word surprised her by not tasting bitter.

The candles lifted their flames in a small shared movement though no breeze passed. Elena noticed his gaze linger on the light as people linger on loved ones. His fingers hovered, not touching the air, but arranging it.

"You're... different," she said, which was, in context, nearly a proposal.

Julian smiled without teeth. "You could say that."

They became friends in an unusual way, starting in the middle. Coffee instead of wine. Walks by the river instead of crowded rooms. She told him she had once imagined moving to the coast, renting a small studio with a box of thyme in the window; how she sometimes woke feeling as if a thought in her head didn't belong to her. He just nodded, like someone who had seen the same thing.

He revealed his nature slowly. Salt scattered at his doorway—not in a line like on television, but in a soft curve, more blessing than blockade. Juniper berries kept in a small pouch in his pocket, rolled between his fingers before a hard conversation. A whisper into the flame of a match before blowing it out. Not theatrics, not spectacle. Just small, everyday practices, woven into the corners of life.

One evening, he reached into the stubborn shrub that grew in the weedy verge near the river path and pinched a sprig free. "Rosemary," he said, placing it in her palm. "Protection. Also, roast potatoes."

She laughed before she realized it might be rude, then slipped the sprig into her coat pocket. For a few steps, the night felt smoother, the shadows less demanding.

Then came the final break. Elena had thought she was being two-timed—that kind of arithmetic she could almost accept, especially since it wasn't another woman but Julian, who had only ever loved men, and toward whom she felt an unexpected pull of friendship. But Damien was never content with tidy sums. His affections spread like geometry gone wild, angles skittering in every direction, a stain seeping into everything it touched. He was impossible to escape. They were both deceived, and Damien already had another conquest waiting in the wings.

Julian's calm finally broke open enough to show what had been holding it. "He won't stop," he said, his voice quiet. "He pulls people in, chews through them, moves on. And we all just... let him."

"He'll ruin himself," Elena said, surprised at how tired her own mouth sounded. "That's what men like that do."

"Not fast enough," Julian said, and there was a spark in it—dangerous, yes, but also clean. "I could help him along. A nudge. So the world might see him for what he is."

"You mean magic," Elena said, the word small, a stone dropped into deep water. Naming it was a way to leash it, to make it less than it was. She had worn the word *witch* in private, but never spoken it aloud, never immersed herself as Julian had. To say it now felt perilously close to summoning.

Julian offered her a place to stay, a way to step fully out of Damien's shadow. He said it lightly, but she heard the weight beneath it. A refuge. She arrived with Ozzy in his carrier and a single bag, repeating to herself it would only be for a night or two—as though brevity could disguise the truth of leaving.

He didn't deny the gravity of what she carried with her. He didn't dramatize it either. That was why she believed him.

That night, in Julian's apartment, his table became an altar. He cleared it without flourish, spread a square of black cloth, and set out jars that had once held jam but now cradled herbs, oils, and darker things. A bowl of salt. A dish of water. A shard of obsidian that caught the candlelight like a secret.

"You don't have to watch," he told her, which was an error.

"I don't trust what happens if I don't," she replied, pulling her knees onto the couch as though to make herself smaller. Ozzy padded from his carrier and curled under the coffee table, his eyes green as embers, as if conscripted into the atmosphere.

Julian worked with the patience of someone arranging grief. Three black candles stood in a row, their wax stubs scarred from other nights. One was phallic in nature, and made Elena glance away, though Julian handled it without embarrassment, winding black thread tight around its base until the wax began to flake.

He anointed each candle with oil from a small brown vial, smearing it along the length in deliberate strokes. The smell rose at once — not the kitchen-warm scent she expected from rosemary, but something sharper, camphorous, antiseptic, as if rosemary had been turned bitter against itself. It caught in her throat, stung her nose, like medicine meant to cauterize rather than heal.

Pins and needles lay scattered like tiny bones across the cloth. He pressed some into the wax until the candles bristled, their shadows jagged on the wall. Beside them, a jar of vinegar and chili stung the air with sour heat, its fumes catching in her nose and making her eyes smart.

He split a pickle, its brine slicking his fingers, and pressed dried vervain inside before binding it back together with twine. "To sour his hunger," he said simply, the vinegar dripping onto the cloth, leaving a sharp stain that burned the air. He set the pickle aside to sag and wither.

The obsidian shard lay at the center, swallowing the candlelight and giving nothing back. Julian placed a photograph beneath a small jar crammed with herbs, then sealed it with wax. The glass caught the light faintly, as though glowing from within. "To trap him in himself."

He lit the candles one by one. The wicks flared, spat, then steadied into thin spears of flame.

"Watch," he told her.

They sat shoulder to shoulder, staring into the fire. The pins glinted, small thorns caught in wax, shadows stretching long across the table. The smell of vinegar and chili was acrid, rising with the waxy smoke, until the air itself seemed to sting. Elena felt her breath fall into rhythm with the flames, the pull and sway of something older than language.

Julian whispered Damien's name once, then again, until the syllables thinned to air. Elena didn't repeat it, but the name was in her blood all the same, pulsing with every beat of her heart. Then came older words, a prayer to Hecate, spoken low and certain.

The nearest candle hissed. Wax spat against the cloth, leaving a blackened circle that smoked faintly. The obsidian reflected all three flames, tripling them into a small, unnatural fire.

"Send it out," Julian said softly, his eyes never leaving the light.

Elena let her gaze sink deeper into the fire until the room around her was gone. The flames blurred, opened, became a tunnel. She pushed the image of Damien into it—his laugh too loud, his lies like hooks—and felt the heat catch. The fire seemed to inhale and carry it away.

For a moment, the whole room leaned. The candles guttered in unison, then burned higher, straighter, as though the work had been accepted.

They sat in silence until the last hiss of wax cooled and the obsidian dulled back into stone. Only then did Julian lean back, his voice low.

"It's gone," he said. "Now it waits to find him."

Elena folded her arms tight across her chest. She didn't answer. She didn't need to. The air already felt lighter, but also emptier, as if something had been sent out into the night and the night had agreed to take it.

Several days passed without a word. Then the call came. Damien's voice was frayed, urgent. He wanted to meet them both at the bar. How he knew they were friends was a mystery to Elena.

When they arrived, Damien was already at the bar, hunched over an untouched drink. His shirt was creased, his hair mussed, and the brilliance he usually wore like cologne had dulled.

He started talking before they sat, his voice too loud for the quiet corner. "Car broke down this morning. Coffee machine at work exploded. Microwave sparked. Every bloody streetlight dies when I walk under it." He gave a brittle laugh and looked from Elena to Julian, waiting for their disbelief, their sympathy, the usual crowding-in of attention.

But the bartender, polishing glasses at the far end, cast him only a flat, withering glance. A woman at the next table shifted her chair slightly away. Where once he would have commanded the room, now it was clear the room was resisting him.

"It's like the whole world's against me," Damien said, eyes darting between them.

Julian didn't bother to answer. He only smirked, the faintest twist of his mouth, and flicked a glance at Elena. The gesture was small, almost careless—but Damien saw it.

His face tightened. Comprehension flickered, then hardened into anger. "It's you," he hissed, half-rising from his chair. "You're doing this to me."

The bartender raised an eyebrow. A couple nearby looked over with mild irritation. No one rallied to him.

Damien scraped his chair back so hard it shrieked against the floor. He stormed out, leaving the drink, the suspicion, and the accusation hanging like smoke in the air.

Later that night, as Elena and Julian turned onto his street, the quiet fractured. Headlights cut across the pavement in a sudden, blinding sweep. An engine roared too loud for the hour, too fast for the narrow block. Brakes screamed. The car shuddered to a halt sideways, tires burning the air.

Damien spilled out before the engine had finished grinding down, the driver's door yawning behind him like a wound that refused to close. His face was raw, stretched tight, lit in harsh slices by the streetlamps. The quiet they'd carried home was gone, stripped away by his arrival.

"You think I don't know?" he shouted, voice ragged enough to grate against brick. He bent, grabbed a rock from the curb, and hurled it at Julian's car. The windshield took it and webbed instantly, a white shocked pattern that caught the moon.

"Damien—" Elena began as if she could somehow stop him.

Another rock whistled past her shoulder and shattered against the building, bits of masonry placing themselves on the sidewalk like a calendar of bad decisions.

"You cursed me!" Damien's voice cracked into a child's wail and then remembered it had an audience. "Everything's falling apart because of you. Both of you. My car, my work—hell, even my own body won't work the way it should." His face flushed as the words tumbled out, humiliation and fury colliding. He brandished another stone, which had the bad manners to be smaller than his previous effort, and moved forward like gravity owed him a favor.

Julian stepped in front of Elena without looking like he meant to. His palms lifted, not in surrender but in quiet command. "You did this to yourself," he said. The words were barely above a breath, yet the night seemed to take them up and carry them outward.

Damien lunged, hurling the stone from too close—anger makes poor mathematicians. For a split second it flew true, then the air itself snapped, sharp as static with a mind behind it. The stone jerked mid-flight, veering as if swatted aside by something unseen. It smacked against the pavement at Damien's own feet, chips of concrete jumping up to sting his shins. He stumbled back, startled, as though the night had turned on him.

The streetlamps winked out one by one, as if called to blackout in a language only wires know. For a moment the world was stage dark. Elena thought—saw?—the dark around Damien drag as if it had hands.

"Enough," Julian said, and it sounded like a verdict.

Damien made a sound she had never heard him make—for the first time, he sounded afraid. He looked at the cracked windshield and flinched at his own reflection: not one face but a dozen, each broken shard inventing an expression. He threw the last rock; it clattered into the gutter without ambition.

"Go home," Julian said, and it was a dismissal, but also, Elena thought, a mercy. Damien backed toward his open car door.

He did not return. Word traveled in fragments and then assembled itself from other people's lips. A shouting match at his office that ended with security lifting their eyebrows and escorting him past a cluster of plants that looked relieved. A small accident on the highway—no one hurt, but his car explained to him that it was tired. Debts he had hidden from himself erupted into print. The new girlfriend disappeared without a word from his life.

No one mentioned curses. Everyone mentioned bad luck. The city prefers luck; it can be pitied without being understood.

Elena and Julian did not celebrate. They sat in the quiet and let adrenaline throb its last. The windshield of his car remained broken, a spiderweb refusing to be erased. They could have called someone then, laid claim to the practical.

"You got what you wanted," Elena said at last.

Julian shook his head. "Not what I wanted. What was bound to happen." He rubbed at the ink near his cuticle. "He was a mirror. We just—" He gestured toward the street, the moon, the arrangement of the night. "We just turned on the light."

Potatoes for the Dead

The kitchen steamed with oil and onion. Outside, Melbourne rain threaded down the glass in thin, steady lines.

Anna flipped the last placki onto the platter. They sighed as they landed, edges crisping to lace. The air was heavy with fried potato, sour cream, and dill. On the bench waited bowls of pierogi glossed with butter, jars of pickles bright under the light, and rye bread still warm from the oven.

Her father would have liked this. He'd come to Australia after the war with nothing but a dented photograph and a pillow hidden in the bottom of a false-bottomed bag. She never asked why he'd brought it — whether it was comfort, or habit, or just the softest thing he owned. She remembered his hands most of all: broad, worn, the lines on his palms nearly vanished, as if work and washing had erased them. He slicked back his dark hair every morning, even when there was nowhere to go. And those blue eyes — piercing, steady, a reminder that he had once stared down men who thought he was beneath them. He never lost his accent. Even now, she could hear it in her head when she peeled potatoes: clipped consonants, that roll of r's and the w that would become a v on words like Wednesday.

She'd told her friends tonight was a "Dumb Supper" — a meal eaten backward and in silence to honour the dead. None of them had heard of it. "Sounds like something out of a folk-horror film," Ben had joked on the group chat. He'd promised to bring wine.

Now the table was set in the narrow dining room. Candles guttered in mismatched holders. A plate sat waiting at the head of the table, untouched. The order of courses was reversed: sweet first, savoury last. A small slice of poppyseed cake waited beside the pickles, the combination faintly absurd and a little sacred.

The doorbell rang.

Ben was first, rain still jewelling his jacket. "If I can't talk, can I at least hum?" he said, grinning as he stepped inside.

"You'll ruin it," Anna replied. "Silence is part of the spell."

Behind him came Lila, shawl tight around her shoulders. She pressed a small loaf into Anna's hands. "Bread for the ancestors," she whispered. "My grandmother used to leave it by the kitchen window."

A few close friends came — people who knew her well enough not to ask too many questions. Ben brought a bottle of red; Lila carried the small loaf like an offering. Someone else had made a salad no one would touch. Their laughter filled the house for a while, light but uncertain, until Anna dimmed the lights and gestured for them to sit.

The room hushed. Forks scraped faintly. The smell of fried potatoes turned heavy, almost sweet. Candlelight gilded the pickles until they looked like trapped emeralds.

Anna raised her glass, turned it once in her hand, and took the first sip. The others followed, uncertain.

They began to eat.

The placki were still warm, the sour cream cool against the tongue. Crunch, hiss, sigh. The sounds were too loud in the hush. Ben tried not to laugh and nearly choked on a bite, earning a sharp look from Lila.

Halfway through her first plate, Anna tasted something she hadn't added — smoke, maybe, or the faint bitterness of burnt wood. The air shifted. The rain outside changed its rhythm. Somewhere near the back door came a sound like boots moving in time.

A faint scent drifted through the room — not food, not candlewax, but the faint sweetness that used to follow her father home: soap, hair oil, polish, and the warmth of his coat after rain. It brushed past her so lightly she almost mistook it for imagination.

She set down her fork, her throat tightening.

The chair at the head of the table stayed empty, but the space around it felt different — filled, somehow, as though the air had changed shape.

No one else seemed to notice at first. Then Ben glanced up from his plate, fork hovering. His expression faltered, the grin slipping from his mouth as though forgotten mid-joke. Lila sat utterly still, her fingers curled around the stem of her glass. The others stared down at their plates, waiting for someone else to move first. The silence, already heavy, seemed to grow a skin.

The scent lingered just above the table now, threaded with something colder — iron, damp wool, the ghost of ration soup. Anna swallowed hard, and the taste of potato shifted in her mouth: it was thinner, plainer, almost raw — like the way he'd described it once, a memory of hunger pressed into starch.

Her father hadn't spoken often about his childhood, but when he did, the memories lingered. He told her about the pear and apple trees that once lined the streets, how he and his brother would climb the branches to pick fruit warm from the sun, juice running down their wrists. Then came the darker stories — the day the Germans arrived in trucks, calling out names, and how they ran until running no longer mattered. He told her how his best friend was shot beside him — one step away, no warning — and how, later, working on a farm, hunger drove him to bite into a raw potato. The farmer caught him and whipped him for it. Things that sent a chill down her spine and couldn't be imagined today.

Now, as her friends sat frozen in their places, a sound rose beneath the silence — a faint, uneven rhythm, as though the room itself remembered what he once endured.

One of the candles flickered, guttered, and then straightened again without wind. The light trembled across the plates. The sour cream had started to melt into the placki, running in pale rivulets that looked almost like wax.

Ben's eyes darted toward the empty chair, then back to Anna. His lips parted, but no sound came — he remembered, she thought dimly, that silence was the rule. Lila's gaze was fixed on the far wall, as though she could see something the rest of them couldn't.

Anna's breath hitched. Her hands had gone cold. Somewhere inside that stillness, she felt it — not sight or sound, but *presence*: the weight of him, the shape of how he'd sat, the way his sleeves always smelled faintly of machine oil. She didn't dare look up, afraid that the illusion, whatever it was, might dissolve.

The smell of burning oil crept stronger, mingling with fried potatoes and candle smoke. A low creak came from the floorboards beneath the chair, like someone shifting their weight.

No one moved. No one breathed.

Anna closed her eyes and saw him as she remembered — his hands broad and lined, the faint shine in his dark hair, the way he'd lean back after a meal with a sigh that seemed to come from somewhere deep.

She wanted to tell him she'd made it just the way he liked, that she'd remembered. But the rules forbade words, and she understood now why: the air was thick with something fragile, a balance that could break if spoken into.

Outside, the rain had stopped. The silence pressed harder.

Then, without warning, the empty glass shifted a fraction, its rim brushing the plate beside it. The sound was small, but every head turned.

The sound was small, but every head turned.

Lila's eyes filled with tears. Ben's mouth hung open, though no sound escaped. Someone stifled a cry — or a laugh — she couldn't tell which.

Anna didn't move.

The empty chair remained what it had always been: wood and air.

And yet—she could have sworn she heard him exhale.

The sound faded as softly as it had come. The rain began again, slow and steady, as though the world had remembered itself.

Anna stared at her plate. The placki had cooled, their edges darkened to bronze. The sour cream had lost its shine. When she lifted her fork again, it felt heavier than before, as if she were eating not food but remembrance.

Around her, no one spoke. Ben set down his fork, carefully, the scrape of metal on china sounding almost like a sigh. Lila reached across the table as if to touch Anna's hand, then stopped herself, uncertain of the rule.

Anna closed her eyes. The warmth of the kitchen pressed around her — the hiss of the stove cooling, the soft breath of the rain, the faint tremor of a tram passing outside. And beneath it all, a pulse of gratitude, memory, and something she couldn't name.

When she opened her eyes, the air felt lighter. The heaviness had gone.

The candle nearest the empty chair sputtered, flared once, and went out.

No one spoke. They didn't need to. The silence now was no longer part of the ritual — it was reverence, fragile and full.

Anna rose first. She gathered the plates, her hands trembling only slightly, and carried them to the sink. The scent of oil still hung in the air, but faint now, threaded with something gentler — a trace of soap, hair oil, and the warmth of his coat after rain.

From the dining room came the slow shuffle of chairs, the uncertain clink of glasses. Someone finally whispered, "Did anyone else...?" but let the sentence trail away.

Anna smiled faintly, not turning. "He was here," she said softly, to the steam rising from the sink, to the rain, to the quiet. "That's enough."

Outside, the rain fell in steady rhythm, washing the night clean.

And then, from somewhere near the open window, came a sound so small she almost missed it — a single, sweet trill. A canary perched on the sill, feathers slicked from the rain, head tilted as if listening.

Anna froze. Her father had kept birds once — bright, whistling creatures that filled his weekends with song. She hadn't seen a canary in years.

It stayed there a moment, its chest puffing with another soft note, before it shook itself, scattering droplets like sparks, and flew off into the night.

Anna stood for a long time, watching the space it had left.

The canary's song melted into the rain, leaving only its echo in the air. Anna turned off the light and felt, for the first time in years, that the house was not empty after all. The night felt gentler now, as if something had been set right.

The Blue Wren

The van had started as a promise. Turquoise paint, a hand-lettered sign, a short menu she could recite in her sleep. No boss. No clocking in. Just coffee, a crowd if she could find one, and air that smelled different every morning. Ivy liked that a life might be built from small, hot cups passed across a counter.

Reality was slower. She learned the dogs' names before their people. Rain smudged the chalkboard. The ledger stayed red no matter how carefully she counted coins. When the generator hiccupped, it felt personal. When wind got under the hatch and rattled it against the latch, the van became a mouth chattering with cold.

Most weekdays she backed into one of the signed food-truck bays along the St Kilda foreshore, near the Esplanade. She liked the same spot beneath a broad-limbed plane tree that threw shade over the hatch by late morning—a habit more than a shelter. Joggers kept their pace; office workers on the tram side kept their eyes. Turquoise flaked at the edges, showing older paint. The previous owner had sold toasties and hot dogs. He'd shaken her hand, warned her about the roof. She kept the warning and painted over the history.

The morning it changed, a mist hung low where grass met path. Ivy could taste it: damp and metallic and thin. She arrived early, set out the chalkboard. *The Blue Wren* in careful script, and beneath it: long black / flat white / latte / mocha / hot chocolate.

A man in hi-vis bought the first long black, paid exact, said nothing. A child bought a hot chocolate, two hands on the lid, asking about marshmallows. Not standard—but she kept a tiny bag for bribes. Between those, she cleaned the steam wand, refilled milk, and checked her phone to be sure she had it right: *Trent. 2pm. Cash buyer if the van's in good shape.* Each time she reread it, the idea of selling opened a gap inside her that looked like relief and failure in equal measure.

At nine-thirty, drizzle started—too light for umbrellas, too insistent to ignore. She pulled the hatch down against the drizzle. The machine sighed as it held pressure, the scent of ground coffee warm against the cold air. She wiped the counter, checked the milk, and waited for the next brave customer.

The old woman arrived without walking toward the van. One moment the path was empty; the next, she was there. Her jacket was long and salt-faded, the kind of canvas that had known years of wind and sea air. The seams were neatly mended, small stitches running straight and sure. Her hair was the colour of linen left too long in the sun. She leaned her elbows on the counter like someone prepared to stay.

"What can I get you?" Ivy asked—the line that started every day and always felt safe.

The woman didn't look at the menu or the machine. Her gaze dropped to the cup Ivy had just pulled, thin curls of steam twisting above the crema.

"Not what you get me," she said. "What you give them. Stir it *against the sun*. Three times. Then listen."

Ivy had heard all kinds of advice. Sprinkle cinnamon. Tap the group handle—*or as the Americans call it, the portafilter*—twice for luck. This was different—less charm, more command. Like a crossing guard: wait here; go now.

"Against the sun?"

"Counterclockwise." The woman tipped her chin toward the cup.

Ivy could have laughed it off, but she was tired and decided to oblige the elderly. She picked up the small spoon she used for stirring sugar and lowered it into the cup. The crema resisted, delicate as skin. She turned her wrist: once, twice, three times against the sun.

The smell didn't get stronger; it got specific. Warmth with citrus. Smoke with something clean. Steam slipped through the service window as if the morning had called it.

A jogger slowed, head turning, laughing like he'd remembered a joke. A woman in a green coat changed direction and walked straight to the van's counter, eyes searching not the menu but the air. Two teenagers stopped their skateboards at the curb and followed whatever thread had reached them.

The first long black after the stirring: the man cupped it under his nose, sipped, went still. "My grandfather's shed," he said, surprised by his own mouth. "Cedar. Sawdust. He kept an orange on the bench and peeled it slow with a pocketknife." He blinked. "Haven't thought of that in years."

A woman ordered a flat white with almond milk, took a mouthful, then covered her mouth as tears rose. "Sorry," she said, wiping her cheek with her sleeve. "My mother's kitchen. Lemon dish soap. Wobbly table. She kept a magazine under the short leg and forgot it until she needed it."

People filtered in from the path, from the sand, from the foreshore walkway. A queue formed without noise. The mist carried the smell farther than it should have. Ivy kept her hands steady. No extra talk, no explanations. Pull. Texture. Three counterclockwise circles whenever she stirred the milk froth. And she listened. That was new. Usually the work sang through her and left no space. Today it made room for the way people breathed out when heat met their fingers, how shoulders lowered, how memory rearranged faces.

Between orders she looked for the old woman—to ask, to thank, to say *what just happened*—but there was no trail. Only a single brass button lay where her elbows had been. It was scratched and cool.

By noon she'd sold through everything: not just the milk and beans she'd stocked for the day, but the extra bags she kept under the counter for emergencies. The coins in the tip jar were heavy. People pressed notes into her palm with a kind of quiet reverence, as if the moment deserved a gesture. A few left odd things—hairpins, a pressed leaf, a ticket stub. She lined them along the back ledge; pocketing felt wrong, binning worse.

When the last cup went out, she dropped the hatch halfway and leaned into the quiet. Her hands shook from the rush's steady speed. The van smelled like work, and like the morning had meant something.

By two, Trent arrived. He walked around the van like he was appraising a second-hand fridge—tapping panels, crouching to squint at the wheels, making small noises of judgment. He was younger than Ivy expected, hair slicked back with product, the smell of an overpowering cologne following him.

"Didn't tell me it was turquoise," he said, shaking his head. "Looks like an ice-cream van."

"It came this way," Ivy said. "I like it."

"The Blue Wren," he repeated, looking at the sign. He gave a short laugh. "Cute. But this thing needs work and no one wants to buy with a name like that. A colour like this is hard to shift. You'd have to sand it back, repaint, redo the signage. The layout's old-school, too. You've got too much gear for a single operator. Grinder like that? Overkill. Bet it chews power."

He leaned through the service window without asking, glancing around like he already owned the place. "And these fittings—bit rough. You'd want to redo the sealant if you didn't want leaks." He straightened, brushing invisible dust from his jacket. "Honestly, you've done alright keeping it running, but it's not worth what you're asking."

"Oh?" Ivy asked, folding her arms.

"Seven, maybe ten grand tops."

She stared at him. "I'm asking thirty!"

"Yeah." He smiled like he was explaining something simple to a child. "You won't get that. Not for this. But hey—cash today if you're realistic."

"I'll think about it," Ivy said.

"Don't think too long," he said, already walking away. "I'll call you later for your decision."

When he left, the air loosened. Ivy placed a small sold-out sign on the counter, cleaned the machine, and wiped the counters. She turned the brass button the old woman had left in her fingers, then slid it into the drawer with spare sugars and tape.

That night at home she spread the takings on the table — notes, coins, and the day's digital total on her phone. She paid the overdue electricity and gas bills. The balance dipped; her stomach followed, then settled. She poured tea into the storm-grey mug from her mother's kitchen, glaze veined with a fine fault line.

Maybe she didn't need to sell. Her mother used to say it when Ivy couldn't decide. *Choose your tide,* she'd say. *Once you're in, stop fighting the pull.*

She slept lightly and dreamed of people in a row, each holding a cup that steamed without cooling. When they drank, they didn't look younger or older—just more themselves. She woke to magpies and a plain feeling: go early.

Before eight she parked under the she-oak tree. Dew still held to the needles. She wiped fog from the inside of the windows, opened the hatch, fired up the espresso machine, ground beans and made the first latte for herself. She stirred counterclockwise, against the sun. Waited.

This time the smell didn't jump; it unfolded. People arrived in ones and twos, then steady. The boy ordered a hot chocolate and, after one sip, said it smelled like the puppy he missed. A nurse, between shifts, cradled her flat white like a way to rest her hands. She told Ivy, unasked, that she'd misread a chart and couldn't stop hearing the words she'd given the wrong family. "Drink," Ivy said softly—nothing else would help—and the nurse did, and her shoulders lowered a fraction.

Near ten, the old woman stood beside the van again. She didn't order. She watched the way people pressed forward, then lingered. Ivy poured three more cups and spoke without turning.

"Why me?" Ivy asked. Not resentful—just genuinely curious.

The woman's voice came from just below the hatch. "Because I've been watching you," she said. "You listen when people speak. You hand over a cup like it matters who's taking it. You don't rush the work or chase the sale. There's power in that."

Ivy blinked. "Power?"

"The kind that mends instead of takes," the woman said. "Most people don't even feel it, but you do. You don't push; you pour. The van knows it too. I couldn't let someone like that man today take it over."

"Trent," Ivy said quietly.

"Names change," the woman said. "But people like him don't. This place would have gone hollow under him."

Ivy's hands rested on the counter. "I was going to sell. I still might."

"You could," the woman said. "But this van was built for more than trade. It needs someone who understands what it can do. And it needs to stay kind."

"And the stirring?" Ivy asked.

The woman smiled, faint and knowing. "That's just how you open the door. Turning against the sun keeps you awake. It's a way of listening." She placed a small folded packet on the counter. "Thread—for your spoon. For mornings when the world feels heavier than it should."

Inside lay a loop of thread the colour between brass and green. Strong, not pretty.

"Who are you?" Ivy asked.

Someone who remembers what this craft can be," the woman said, and turned down the path toward the sea

By noon, the van was busy and still, filled with its own kind of hush. Ivy tied the thread to the end of her spoon so she could find her way *against the sun* by feel. The spoon clicked softly against the cup each time she stirred.

A man said he'd come because his coffee had smelled like rain on hot concrete—the first storm after a heavy summer. A woman said hers tasted like the back room of the bookshop where she'd had her first job. A girl brought a photo of her father and stood not to drink, but to breathe. "There," she whispered, smiling at nothing Ivy could see.

Ivy didn't try to explain it anymore. She just kept listening.

By the week's end, she'd earned more in seven days than she had in the previous twelve months. Enough to pay her spot fee ahead and still go home with a wallet that felt heavy in her hand. The card reader totals blinked back from her phone like quiet proof.

People waved now when they passed, even if they weren't stopping. Some dropped by just to talk. A man from the florist brought her a single stem each morning—whatever hadn't sold the day before. A mother left a folded drawing from her child: a turquoise van with steam shaped like music. Ivy pinned it near the till.

On Friday, Trent showed up again. His own truck was parked farther along the foreshore—black vinyl, chrome script, and a name that shouted instead of spoke: *GRINDHAUS*. Music thudded from a speaker beside the hatch. The smell of burnt beans drifted up the path.

"Big day, huh?" he said, leaning against Ivy's van. "Council's been down my way—reckon my setup's one of the best they've seen. Real modern look. You should swing by, see how the pros do it."

"I'll take your word for it," Ivy said, passing a latte to a regular who smiled and called her name.

"Still got that old grinder?" Trent asked. "Thing must be chewing power. Tell you what—when you're ready to sell, I'll make you a deal. You could fold this van into my fleet. I'll rebrand it, bring it up to standard. *'GRINDHAUS LITE'* or something."

"That's generous," Ivy said mildly. "But I'm doing alright and don't want to sell at the moment."

He smirked. "Alright's fine—for now. Markets move, though."

A young couple walked past, holding takeaway cups from his truck. The woman took a sip, made a face, and spat discreetly into a napkin. "That's awful," she muttered. The man dropped the cup into a nearby bin without looking back.

Trent saw it too. His jaw tightened. "People don't know what they like until you teach them," he said. "Only way to make a good profit margin is cheap beans."

"Maybe," Ivy said and shrugged.

He ordered one of her coffees, trying to sound casual. Ivy made it the same as every other—steady hand, quiet care. When she slid the cup across, he took a sip, frowned, and set it down.

"That's revolting," he said loudly.

The woman waiting behind him smiled faintly. "Funny," she said. "Mine is always perfect."

Laughter rippled through the line, low and warm. Trent stepped back, muttered something about "different tastes," and walked away. His truck's music faded as he drove off, taking the smell of scorched beans and bad attitude with him.

When the rush eased, Ivy stood in the doorway of the van. The air smelled of salt and milk and warm metal. She ran a finger over the thread tied to her spoon, feeling where it had frayed. Around her, the sounds of the foreshore folded in—wheels on gravel, a gull's cry, the sigh of the she-oaks.

She realised at some point during the week she'd stopped thinking of the van as something she owned. It was something she kept alive.

A man returned a cup she'd lent him earlier, rinsed and clean. "You'll be here tomorrow?" he asked.

"Yes," Ivy said. "Tomorrow."

She turned the sign to *Closed* and watched the reflection of the turquoise paint in the glass, bright even in shadow. She thought of the old woman's words—how turning *against the sun* was setting intention in every cup.

The van hummed as it cooled, a sound like contentment. Ivy smiled, locked up, and walked toward the line of she-oaks, the tide pulling steady and sure beyond them.

The Cinema on the Dust Road

The cicadas were louder than the engine when it finally gave out. One last cough, a juddering rattle that felt personal, then a shiver through the steering column and silence—except for the insects, a crackling choir threaded through the heat. She tried the key again, then a third time, as if stubbornness could coax life from the dry heart of the car. The sound that came back was the tinny click of refusal.

She let her head thump against the wheel and closed her eyes. Her own breath came back at her sour and warm. Dust swam in the sunlight like something alive. She told herself she wasn't afraid—only stranded—and that fear, like water, was a luxury in a place this dry.

Outside, the air hit her like a door. She squinted into the pale sky and felt heat slide across her face, down the column of her neck, into the places a breeze used to live. The road pulled itself tight to the horizon, a strip of film stretched between two blank frames. A wind sock of spinifex made slow circles near the verge. A fresh wedge-tailed eagle lifted from the carcass of a kangaroo and flapped lazily away, leaving the smell behind—sun-warmed iron and sweet rot.

She lifted the bonnet and touched everything that looked like it wanted touching. None of it answered. Eventually, she stepped back, palms filthy, and pretended she'd meant to stop here all along.

It was the kind of day that forgot the existence of shade. A fly crawled beneath her sunglasses and skittered along her cheekbone. She swore softly and sent it away. The silence behind the cicadas deepened as afternoon tilted toward evening, the light going thinner and more yellow, like old newspaper. She told herself she would wait beside the car. Someone would come. A truck. A ranger. A farmer returning to a property invisible from the road. Even a plane would do, low enough that she could wave both arms and make a story later of the way it dipped its wings in answer.

She lasted ten minutes. Then fifteen. Another fly. The heat clung like a hand.

The water was tepid, metallic. She capped the bottle, slung the strap over her shoulder, and walked on.

Gravel muttered under her boots. Red dust crawled up her jeans and settled in the bend of her arms, leaving a salt tang on her lips. The horizon wavered, an endless blank canvas, empty of signs or markers. Panic pressed at her chest. What if no one came? Where was she even heading?

"Nothing to see here," she told no one. "Nothing to see."

Nothing to see, and then—light.

It wasn't the clean stab of a star or the hurtful slice of oncoming headlights. It was warmer than that, steadier, a pulse that didn't so much pierce the air as persuade it. At first, she thought it was the sun caught again, reflected off something that shouldn't be able to reflect in a place like this. But the sun was lowering away to the west, and this new light was ahead, slightly left of the road's seam, a glow growing clearer as the mirage gave it permission to become real.

"Absolutely not," she said, because it helped to hear doubt in her own voice. She kept walking, because it helped more to pretend she hadn't noticed.

The light waited. With every step it unspooled more of itself. The road lifted gently and then dropped, and at the top of the rise she saw it.

A cinema.

Not a shed with a screen. Not a truck with a projector stuttering off the back. A full, unapologetic cinema, its façade pressed with art deco geometry, the ribs of the building gliding into a marquee that chewed up moths in its neon. Letters clung to the frame in a partial announcement:

TONIGHT ONLY

The words hummed. Insects swarmed the bulbs and threw shadows like confetti. A single poster box displayed a glossy image of a woman in soft focus, a tilt to her mouth that said she knew the end before it happened.

She stood in the middle of the road and laughed once. It sounded bright and brittle and almost like the crack of glass. Of course there was a cinema. Out here, where the trees were suggestions and the wind carried nothing but itself, of course there was a marquee offering entertainment, offering cool and dark and seats that would cup you like a hand. Of course there was.

She walked closer because she had already begun to and because the doors breathed open at her approach. When they did, they sighed cool air—conditioned, perfumed faintly with polish and popcorn and something older, something like mothballs and damp velvet. Her whole body, surface to core, reached for it.

The cinema wavered like a mirage, unreal against the dust. Yet it was solid beneath her hand, the only promise of shelter. She let the hesitation slip and went inside.

Carpet took her weight and softened it. The lobby glowed. Chandeliers hung like frozen thunderstorms above her. Sconces fired the walls with warm, circular light. The ticket window gleamed. The concession counter sat behind a crown of glass, its jars filled with sweets the colour of children's afternoons—boiled lollies, mint leaves, milk bottles soft enough to push a tooth into.

A buttery haze of popcorn wrapped her, the kind of smell that belonged to childhood matinees and Saturday afternoons, impossibly alive here.

And then there were the staff. They were not young and they were not old; they were at the age where a face learns what to do and holds itself to it. The usher's jacket fit too well to be anything but tailored. The ticket seller had a bow at the throat that seemed to float above the skin. All three looked up with the same steadied smile, and all three smiles were perfect, if you liked that sort of thing.

"Welcome," the usher said, and the word did not echo because everything in the lobby ate sound. "We've been expecting you."

"I don't understand," she answered lamely.

The ticket seller slid something through the little half-moon cut in the glass. A card. He held it delicately between two fingers. She took it and felt the weight of it, the nap. It was a proper ticket. The ink showed her name in letters that hadn't smudged.

"I didn't buy this."

"Of course not," the concession clerk said in a voice like collar starch. "It's been arranged."

"By who?"

The clerk's smile didn't reach his eyes, not quite. "By the programme."

"There's been a mistake," she said. Panic pressed at her ribs, urging flight, but the air-conditioned calm held her fast. Somewhere behind the glow of the lobby, she imagined, a phone waited.

"Mistakes are for daylight," the usher told her kindly. "Shall we?" He held out an arm, white glove making a brief, precise opening in the air.

She should have said no. She should have made a fuss in ordinary language. But ordinary language had always been flimsy in her mouth, and here it seemed to have no purchase at all, like trying to climb a wall with hands made of water. She followed the usher to the double doors, which opened without being touched, and walked into the cool dark that waited.

The theatre made a body forget its shape. Velvet seats cupped her and dimmed her outline. The screen was a potential more than a presence, a pale sheet of breath waiting to turn into something. The air was cold enough to reach into her shirt and smooth the skin at the small of her back.

She looked around and saw that she was not alone. The seats were full.

The audience, though, did not gather as audiences do. They were not rows of people with faces and phones lit like contraband stars. They were impressions, densities, the suggestion of a shoulder and the slope of a neck without committing to the rest. They flickered, not as failing light flickers but as a memory does when you demand specifics from it. When she glanced at one, it gained features, and when she tried to keep them in her eyes they seemed to change to something else.

The projector breathed and found its voice. The beam cut the air, making a column of dust that looked like rain falling upward. The screen woke and showed a picture that made the first sound in her throat since she'd crossed the threshold.

It was her.

Not an actress chosen for resemblance. Not the trick of a face you see everywhere when grief is fresh.

She was ten months old, hair pale as straw, squinting in a yellow dress. A plastic bucket hung awkward in her hand.

The beach was the one with the long, shallow pool and the jetty that shivered in storms, stonework said to be laid by convicts.

The sand cut her skin; she remembered the sudden sting, the crying, and her father lifting her into his arms. He pressed her close, rinsed her foot in the salt water, his touch steady as if he had always known how to keep her safe.

Recognition came first, warming her with the ache of nostalgia. But beneath it came confusion, then the quiet edge of fear — because she knew this moment, every detail of it, from a still photograph in her mother's collection.

She tasted salt. It felt right. Once, as a child, she had licked her wet wrist and told herself she'd swallowed the ocean. Now, in the seat, memory rose in her throat, briny and sharp.

The film jittered—not from age, but by design. On screen she was older, fourteen maybe, in a yard that smelled of lawn clippings and petrol. She leaned against the weatherboard shed while a boy, all wrists and nerves, stumbled through sentences. Then the kiss: shy, sudden. She felt it on her lips even now, the sweetness of chewing gum, the shock of not being disappointed, the laugh she bit back so he wouldn't mistake it. The picture jumped skyward, then shuddered down again to faces flushed.

A seat to her left creaked. She turned and saw a figure turn back toward her. For an instant the outline gave detail; a profile sharpened, a familiar drop to a nose, a scar that had been with her for as long as she could remember. Her own face looked at her from the seat beside and then blurred back to suggestion as if looking at oneself too directly was vulgar.

The audience breathed like a single animal. The projector changed reels.

Her mother's funeral. Yellow roses like stale butter in the heat. A minister who had loved the sound of his own voice since childhood. The stone cooled her palm. She wanted, with a desperate ordinariness, to climb in after the coffin—if only there were a way back out.

She didn't cry until three days later when the kettle clicked and she was suddenly and completely alone inside a house.

She flinched and swallowed and refused. "Enough," she said. It wasn't loud, but the theatre was made to hear anything addressed to it.

The lights rose like a thoughtful tide. An usher stood at her elbow with his head not quite bowed, a man rehearsed in not interrupting and not waiting either.

"Miss," he said, the word the softest shoulder of sound, "the operator will see you now."

He led her through a door that stayed open just long enough to close behind her and down a corridor that couldn't be the length it was. The cream colored paint peeled not in flakes but in scrolls. The bulbs in the ceiling made a noise like a hive that had decided to stop pretending to be patient.

Stairs. Narrow. She put her hand on the rail and left a damp shape. The air smelled of oil and hot metal and something sweet, a scent like marzipan. She climbed until she felt taller and smaller at once.

The projection booth looked out over the audience like a ship's bridge. From here, the people below were a map of shadows. The window's edge was worn to the colour of old coins. The projector itself was a beast with its hide of chrome and enamel and its throat of light that never swallowed.

He sat in the half-light like a man who had practiced long and hard to be still. The projectionist was neither thin nor robust; he had the kind of shape that implied the body had never made demands and had never been indulged. His skin had the pallor of people who live with machines instead of weather. His hair—if that was hair—lay smooth enough to be lacquered. When he turned to her, she saw eyes the colour of the moment before lightning, and hands that had memorised their positions and kept them.

"These," he said, and his voice had the scrape of paper in it, "are your endings."

He didn't gesture in a grand way; he simply inclined a hand at the wall behind her. She turned, and the breath left her. The shelves ran up and up, a library without books. Reels. Dozens. Hundreds. Some were fat-bellied with film, their spines labelled in a hand as clear and unemotional as a signpost: years, sometimes, and sometimes single words. A few labels had been rubbed—the way a date is rubbed from a headstone when the stone is asked to do too much.

"My endings," she repeated uncertainly.

"All of them," he said. "Well. All of them we have the rights to." His mouth tilted, half-joke, half-rule.

"That's not funny."

"No," he agreed. "It isn't."

He lifted a reel. The label read QUIET in ink that looked freshly dry. He moved with the care of a man who knew how easily things go to flame. He threaded the film with fingers that did not try to hurry, and the projector took it with a sound like breath taken in.

On the booth's far wall, a new screen made itself from old paint. The image was her again but in a room she had not yet furnished. A small lounge where mornings were measured as a ceremony and evenings where a radio was a companion. A neatness to everything that suggested control and also resignation. She was older, not yet old. Her hair had learned to be grey at the edges and keep the rest to itself. She looked—safe.

The image stuttered and showed a Sunday. A friend from work who sometimes sat in the chair by the window and sometimes didn't. A nephew on a visit, quickly bored. Plants in the kitchen that thrived under discipline. A quiet life.

"No," she said softly. It was not disgust, not fear. Just an honest measurement of herself against a particular peace she couldn't wear.

He nodded and lifted another reel. The label said GOLD. The film spat light.

She saw herself standing on a street. The camera—if there was a camera—moved in close as a man moved in closer. His mouth had the kind of smile you could fold a life into. In the next moment the two of them walked into a room that could hold the two of them without argument. A bed. A dinner burnt and eaten anyway. Laughter like two coins struck together and both sounding richer for it. And then—because the reel had not promised anything but its own honesty—the flash of a siren, the vulgarity of sudden grief, a black suit that fit because it had to.

"Love and its fee," the projectionist said without malice.

She shook her head once as if clearing water from her ears. "Next."

He obliged. AMBITION, the label said, and the light did not so much begin as take over. She saw a stage, and herself on it, and a room of eyes all pointed and bright. Her voice was a clean instrument. The feeling of it—that feeling—it made her taller than she was. She held a book that belonged to her and belonged to a thousand hands at once. The applause moved through her like weather. There was a flight, a hotel, four interviews, a day of silence. Then a grip on the shoulder that turned to a grip on the lungs. The camera tore itself into pieces trying to find a place to put the smoke, and she watched herself be carried out of the frame, and the frame struggled to make sense of being empty.

She stepped back as if distance could soften impact. "No."

"Some work costs more," he said. "Some cost is paid in any case."

"Trawl all of them," she said suddenly, a flare of anger giving her orders. "Show me a reel where it doesn't—where I am not a trick with a cruel punchline. Where I get to the end and it is not a... not a lesson."

He considered her face carefully and sighed. "There is no reel without an end," he said. "But their flavours differ." He glanced at the shelves. "Some are bitter up front and sweet in the aftertaste. Some are honeyed until you notice what's on your tongue. Some you drink and find yourself thirsty still. Some you sip and never recover from the smallness of them."

She wondered if it was kinder to face the inevitable, to know how it ended, or if ignorance might be its own mercy. Was it worse to walk blind into what waited, or to live haunted by an ending already etched in film?

"I could leave," she said, and the word leave made a space inside her chest that looked like a door.

He nodded. "Back to the road."

"And then?"

"And then the road returns you to itself," he said. "Which is to say—nothing of note."

She understood then that nothing of note was not the same as safety, and certainly not the same as mercy. Out there, the sun would burn itself out, the air would cool, and the stars would cut their shapes into the dark. She would sit by the car and the night would come with its noises and leave without apology. Maybe morning would deliver help. Maybe it would not. The world, in its size, would not choose to remember her.

She looked again at the shelves. A reel without a year had a label that stuttered between two words—as if the hand that wrote it had changed its mind too late. She reached for it and the projectionist stopped her—not with touch, but with an angle of the hand that suggested the existence of rules.

"That one is not for pre-selection," he said.

"What does it say?"

His eyes flicked to the projector and back again. "HOME," he said at last. "Or HOLLOW, depending on the light."

She gave a short laugh that hurt in her chest. "Of course."

He lifted a reel she hadn't seen him choose. It vibrated faintly in his hands. The label read LAST. With the quiet ease of long practice, he threaded it through the machine. The projector caught and began to turn.

On the wall appeared a room she half-recognised, the way a dream sometimes feels familiar without reason. A window rattled in its frame. On a table sat a cup, cracked but still holding water. She was there—older, steadier—writing a list without names and finding beauty in its spareness. In the yard, a man who was not a stranger trimmed the hedge into its natural shape. A radio muttered the weather as if apologising.

She felt it then: not joy, not despair, but a soft grief, almost companionable, resting in her like an animal asking only to be acknowledged. She wasn't happy in the way magazines promised. She wasn't unhappy either. She looked finished, but not done with.

The screen pulsed. Her hand lifted toward it before she realised.

"Careful," the projectionist said—not as a warning, but like a benediction.

"You said I could choose."

"You've been choosing since you walked in," he said. "This is the moment where choice stops pretending to be a rumour."

She stepped into the narrow slot of the projector's beam. It was warm in the way sunlight is warm on the back of a hand. Dust floated in it, each speck a little planet with a private moon. The reel spun, and in its spins she could almost hear words, not spoken, but arranged into sense: if, if, if, if—

She lifted her hand. The light gathered in her palm like water cupped to drink. It flexed around her fingers as if it had joints. She had a single thought, very clear: that the desert was an honest place because it never promised you more than it could give, and that this, whatever this was, was not honest, but it was... it was kind in the way that a door is kind when it stays unlocked.

Then she pressed her hand deeper and the surface of the light let go of itself and became a softness she fell through.

The noise was back—the insects all at once, the projector, the breath of an audience primed to respond. The light cancelled light. For a moment she could smell everything on earth: the oil that makes machines purr, the lemon of polish, the inside of a cinema seat where countless afternoons had stained the fabric with stories. And then she smelled only starch and something like mothballs and—yes—the faintest sweet almond that made the back of her throat think of danger.

Silence.

When she opened her eyes, the world had composed itself around her with precision.

The lobby waited. The chandeliers held. The carpet shone. The poster woman continued not to smile. Her chest rose and fell in a rhythm that was not quite hers.

She looked down.

The uniform had found her shape with the confidence of a tailor who had measured a body while it slept. The jacket's seams knew where to end. The skirt stopped in a way that kept secrets. A cap perched on her head. Her hands had folded themselves behind her back. She tried to pull them out and they didn't, not because something held them, but because something—her—knew this was where they belonged.

Another staff member passed. She didn't know this face, and yet she knew how to receive the nod: with a tilt that had been practised for a century and didn't need mirrors anymore.

"In place, please," the staff member murmured, and the words did the work of hands on a shoulder, placing without touching. "The next guest is nearly here."

Her mouth prepared the smile. She did not give it permission. It moved obediently anyway. She tried to think of the car on the road, the hot metal ticking as it cooled, the dust keeping its counsel. She tried to think about the version of her that might have sat through a night with the stars chewing on the edge of her courage. The thought tipped, caught, vanished.

Headlights drew a white seam across the glass doors. An engine coughed in the night and fell silent. Outside, cicadas rose in chorus.

The usher lifted a gloved hand. The concession clerk adjusted a cap that seemed to belong less to the person than to the role. She felt the weight of the ticket in her palm and noticed, absurdly, the card stock—the faint tooth of it under her thumb.

The brass handles turned. The doors opened with quiet grace. A traveller stood at the threshold: a woman, about her age, hair loose from its tie, dust shadowing her shin. Her eyes carried the look of someone who hadn't known what to expect, and then been wrong even about that.

This is the moment, she thought. She wanted to say *Don't. Run. There's nothing here you'll be allowed to keep.* She wanted to say a name—hers, the traveller's—say the word that would undo it all. But instead her mouth shaped the sentence that belonged to the building.

"We've been expecting you," she heard herself say. The words came warm, a welcome the woman could step into. There was no argument left in the air.

The traveller's fingers closed over the ticket waiting for her. The staff shifted back into place. Somewhere behind, the projector stirred like a priest at the altar.

She caught her reflection in the poster glass. Not the actress's glossy face, not the ticket seller's neat bow, but her own outline—pale, precise, rehearsed. A kindness shaped as a trap. The reflection smiled. It looked natural. It would, she thought, with practice.

The doors whispered shut. The carpet swallowed footsteps. The building cooled as if a breath had been released.

Outside, the desert folded into night. Inside, the reels waited—tender, merciless as weather.

She stood where the role had placed her. The lights were perfect. A faint marzipan note lingered in the air, then vanished.

A fly tapped at the glass and then fell. The usher cleared his throat, the sound almost gracious.

On the other side of the doors, the theatre breathed in.

She held the next ticket without looking at the name. She knew, as surely as knowing how to stand, that she would speak again when the time came, and the sentence would be waiting, and another traveller would walk forward, and the light would take them in.

Witch of Malfunction

The café faltered the instant Marin stepped inside.

The playlist snagged on the same half-line and stammered three times before surrendering to a hush that made the air feel thick. The card reader held a single, reproachful tone—a prolonged beep that sounded more like a complaint than a function. Steam hissed from the espresso machine in uneven bursts, the groan of tired pipes, the memory of something scorched on a stove.

Sweetness hung in the room, cloying and acrid at once, as if someone had caramelized a mistake and let it burn. Beneath it lay a faint metallic tang, the scent of singed wiring that clung to the throat like an unspoken warning. Most customers tensed at the first glitch and turned for the door with a mutter about broken places and unreliable staff. Marin never did. The friction in the air had always pulled at her.

Her coffee waited on the far corner of the counter, set there by a barista who'd stopped asking questions months ago. It was easier to have it ready before she crossed the threshold. The screen froze less that way, and the apologies didn't stack up in the space between them like used cups.

She took the mug with a small nod. The girl at the register tried for a smile and didn't quite make it. Around them, the café breathed in fits: a ceiling bulb pulsed and steadied; the ice machine clicked once like a swallowed argument; a drip from the espresso wand gathered itself into a trembling globe but would not fall.

Her table waited beneath a single lamp that trembled though no air stirred. The scattered chairs suggested others had tried to settle there and failed. Marin took the corner seat—the one facing the long window where rain traced bright lines before abandoning its script halfway down the glass. Steam from her coffee drifted upward, clinging to the bent metal shade above her, pale and hesitant, like a breath that refused to leave the body.

She stirred counterclockwise, a banishing habit she'd picked up decades ago. Porcelain touched spoon and rang a crisp, precise note. It traveled farther than it should have, beyond her table into the hollow spaces, as if someone had cupped a hand to the sound and carried it to the corners. The hair along her arms lifted. She felt watched, but not with eyes. The room had a mood. It had always had one. Today it felt like something hovering just out of reach.

A laugh slipped across the floor from the table towards her left—low, measured, unhurried. Not the distracted sound of a feed-scroller. The sort of laugh that comes on cue.

She looked up without turning all the way. The man sat in uneven light, half his face pulled into angles by the bulb overhead. He cradled a mug in both hands and didn't drink. The faintest curve touched his mouth, and then it was gone.

"You notice it," he said.

Not a question. His voice was careful, pitched to take nothing from her and offer nothing she hadn't asked for.

Marin let the spoon rest against the rim. "Places get unsettled," she said. "Some more than others."

"Unsettled." He tasted the word and set it down as if on a saucer. "You seem to have that effect."

The card reader on the counter let out a sharp chirp in response. The barista flinched, pressed a button that did nothing, and turned it off and on again the way one pacifies a petulant appliance.

He watched the bulb above her seat tremble. "It's one thing to notice it, but it changes once it knows who you are — once it recognizes you, you can't just walk away."

Marin didn't answer, though her pulse let her know it heard him. The steam from her coffee curled toward the bulb and held there, coiling itself around the metal lip. She traced the handle of her mug with her fingertip and found heat in the ceramic like held breath.

He took a sip that wasn't a sip. "It listens when you stir," he said. "You anchor it without meaning to."

"You're very certain," she said, still not looking at him and shaking her head.

"Mm." His agreement felt like a small door left ajar. "Certainty's a big word. Recognition is smaller. Easier to carry."

Silence thinned between them, not unfriendly. She counted the seconds by the clicks of some hidden mechanism

in the machine behind the bar: five clicks and a hiss, five clicks
and a hiss. A rhythm just shy of calm.

The sugar bowl on the table rattled, a small percussion
that made the barista lift her head and frown. The spoon in
Marin's cup trembled in place, tapping porcelain without her
hand on it. She closed her fingers around the handle by reflex
and the trembling stilled, as if chastened.

The printer at the register woke again like a startled bird. It
whirred, choked, and spat a receipt so violently the barista
swore and snatched at it. The girl wadded the slip in her fist,
eyes darting, and shoved it under the till.

Too late. She'd already glimpsed her name— MARIN
–letters so clean they stung.

She said nothing. The man said nothing. The café said
nothing, and the silence thickened until it seemed to stop the
room.

Light faltered. A drop of rain slid halfway down the glass
and stalled, silver against the day. A door in the back exhaled
and stayed ajar. Voices broke off mid-sentence, mouths still
shaping words but without sound.

The café held its breath.

The barista froze mid-motion, cups poised in her hands.
At the window, a man hovered over his pastry bag, fingers
suspended just above the paper. Even the rain on the glass had
turned into a painting.

Only Marin and the man stood outside the frozen
moment. His eyes held hers, steady, attentive, without demand.

"It isn't broken," he said. "I think it wants something."

Her throat tightened, though she kept her face composed. "It's dramatic," she said, dryly. "Some places like an audience."

Something flickered across his face—agreement, maybe even respect. "Some places are tired of not being heard."

The sugar bowl tapped against the table, this time deliberate. She spilled a drift of crystals, nudging them into a ring until the grains caught the weak light.

"Enough," she whispered—not to him, not exactly to the room, but to the presence within it.

The pendant light steadied. The hiss behind the counter dropped into a sigh.

Then the printer spat again, the noise so sharp it made her teeth ache. Time resumed its normal pace and the cafe patrons were non the wiser to what had just occurred.

HURT.

The word marched down the slip of paper in a font that tolerated no argument. The barista reached for it, saw the letters, and let her hand fall.

Marin stepped forward and took the receipt instead. Her fingers closed around it, and it felt warmer than it should have. The paper thrummed against her skin like a plucked wire, like something alive that had borrowed the body of a receipt.

The letters landed in her chest like a bruise. The room's heat pressed close, a damp cloth thrown over her shoulders. She moved to the counter and set her palm on the metal ledge where hands had knocked coins and elbows for years. The surface pulsed faintly against her skin. Not a vibration—a heartbeat that didn't belong to anything with blood.

"Show me," Marin whispered, the words almost breath

Screens along the back bar flickered. For a moment they showed only their own reflections: light and shadow, Marin's hand against the metal, the barista's wide eyes. Then the reflections fractured, and impressions shook loose. Not photographs, not quite memories, but the kind of truths a place keeps when no one is listening.

Paint peeling where leaks had streaked the ceiling. A floor mopped with gray water and left sticky underfoot. A sink dripping into a bucket until the bucket overflowed. Wires stripped and bound with tape that peeled back like old scabs. Corners where dust gathered into small, ignored monuments.

And the owner's voice, too easy with laughter, spilling from a phone on speaker: *If a café has to fail at something, let it fail theatrically. People like a story. They'll forgive a story quicker than they'll forgive the prices.* A pause, then his grin made sound: *Haunted. Say haunted. It'll sell.*

Other calls, other words. *Developers have an eye on the block. Once I get a decent offer, I'll let the whole place go. Doesn't matter if the pipes burst or the lights give out. Someone else will pay to tear it down.*

The visions pressed against Marin's chest like a bruise. This wasn't charm or character. It was neglect dressed up as atmosphere, a home left to rot while its owner polished the story of its ruin. The café had been made into a mask, a joke. And it was tired of being laughed at.

The machines hissed beneath the vision, every sound edged with overwork. She tasted metal on her tongue.

Marin closed her eyes and steadied her breath before she opened them again.

The man had not moved. He watched her hand on the metal with an attention that held steady but did not intrude.

"It chose you," he said. No drama in it, no flourish. Just fact. "Because you listen."

The words struck her deeper than they should have. Listening had always cost something. Some days it cost most of her. She looked at him fully then, and in his stillness she saw it—the same awareness, the same refusal to look away when the world bent sideways. He hadn't frozen with the others because he couldn't. He was like her.

Her thumb moved over the counter in a slow line. She shook the last of the sugar out into a neater circle—not a ritual, not quite—and flattened it with her palm until the crystals formed a thin, bright boundary.

"No more fits," she told the cafe. "Not like this." The tone she used for skittish dogs and children on the edge of throwing something heavy. "You have my attention. I can help you."

The lights above the register lowered and lifted in something like a nod. The air slackened its hold. The door opened with its usual bell that had never learned to ring properly and always sounded like a cough. Keys jingled. The owner entered with his phone to his ear and the look of someone already rehearsing annoyance.

He walked three steps in and the card reader shrieked like a kettle pushed too hard. The bulbs along the bar dropped to a glower and rose together, not a malfunction but an answer. Shadows in the corners drew closer to the walls and held there, shoulders braced.

He paused. One hand went flat against his chest, as if his own heartbeat had reminded him of something he'd forgotten. "What now," he said to no one, and then—louder, into the phone—"Yeah, yeah, it's doing it again, the thing, I told you we should lean into it, people—"

The voice on the other end rose like static. The room tightened.

She felt the café gather itself, the way a child gathers itself before the wail that will unhouse everyone within earshot. It pushed against her palms where they rested on the counter. The push wasn't rage.

She nodded once, barely more than breath. "Let go," she said, under the hum. "I will handle this now."

The espresso machine hissed in approval. The air leaned.

The owner staggered. Not the stumble of a man losing balance. The grip-and-release of someone feeling a hand at the center of his back urging him on. He looked at the door as if it were farther away than it had been, eyes watery with confusion. "Hey," he said, and didn't know who he was saying it to. He took one step toward the exit, then another. His shoulders hunched as though against weather that hadn't reached anyone else.

"Sir?" the barista said, the word shrinking in the air as soon as it left her mouth.

He turned his head and looked over his shoulder. For a moment his expression bared itself—bafflement without cruelty, shock without comprehension. Not a man punished, exactly. He looked bewildered, as though the café itself had turned against him. His gaze flicked past the barista, past the man at the table, past Marin, as if searching for someone in charge who could explain. She kept her palms on the counter. Her hands were steady now.

The bulbs along the bar warmed. The door, which had stuck for a week, opened easily when the owner reached it. He paused with the threshold at his shoulder, the rain cutting a silver sheet inches from his shoes. His mouth twitched into the beginning of a protest that never found its words.

He kept walking.

The door shut with a softness that felt like a full stop. The bell made its cough. The room exhaled in a sigh so long and low she felt it in her knees.

Silence held for a beat, then broke gently under the weight of ordinary things: a spoon against ceramic, a throat clearing, the shuffle of shoes. People looked at one another with the muzzled smile of those who suspect they have missed something important and politely agree not to mention it. The barista leaned on the counter with both hands and let out a laugh without knowing why.

The observant man set his mug down on the table and walked toward her.

He studied her for a long moment, then said what she had been refusing to admit.

"You've been ignoring it. Pushing it down. Tonight you stopped pretending. You found it."

The barista's gaze flicked between them, then settled on the counter where Marin's hands still rested. Her expression softened into something like relief. She gave a small nod—the kind a person gives their boss without thinking.

And in the barista's eyes there was no trace of the man who had stood here an hour ago. The memory of him had thinned to nothing, replaced by a certainty that Marin had always been the boss. Around them, conversation resumed in the cautious, steady way of a room returning to itself. No one questioned the shift. No one asked for signatures or explanations. The café had chosen, and the people within it moved with the ease of those who had never believed otherwise.

Marin lifted her mug. It had cooled without losing heat. The first mouthful tasted like something relieved of a weight it hadn't known how to drop. The bulbs above cast a warmer circle. The hiss from the machine had become a hum pitched to settle, like a cat making peace with a lap.

"The receipts," she said softly, almost to herself, "they weren't warnings. They were instructions."

The man's mouth curved at that, but he didn't press. He didn't need to.

Marin set the mug down and brushed sugar from her palm. "Tomorrow," she said, her voice steady now, "we fix the wiring. Patch the leaks. Replace the bucket with one that doesn't cut into the fingers. New tape, proper tape. Fresh paint. And the floor—no more sticky steps."

The barista let out a breath that turned into a laugh, one that belonged to someone who believed their shift might end without apology.

Magic had claimed the place. Care would keep it.

The man regarded her, and this time his smile stayed. "Most of us," he said, "get flickers. Sparks. A handprint on a fogged window, if we're lucky. You got a voice. And now"—his gaze flicked to the counter where her hand still rested—"you've got a place."

Marin met his eyes, unflinching. "For now," she said. Her hand pressed once against the wood, a quiet seal. "And tomorrow, it will be better."

Overhead, the bulbs dipped and rose together, not a malfunction but an assent. The hum of the machine softened into something like a purr, steady and low, the sound of a place that had decided it could rest.

Between Shadows and Saints

Rachel's hands shook as though the river had already seeped into her veins. Was she doing the right thing?

"Momma?" Evie whispered, her small fingers curling into Rachel's. The girl's blue eyes were steady, clear, as if they carried more years than she had lived.

"Everything will be just fine," Rachel said, though her voice trembled.

The boat loomed above them, black and hulking, smoke furling from its stacks like incense to a god she wasn't sure was listening. It seemed less a vessel than a beast waiting to swallow them. She lifted Evie and felt again the strange calm the child always gave off, a warmth that quieted the hammering of her heart. Rachel clutched that warmth as though it were divine.

They boarded, weaving through clusters of passengers until they reached the rail. Rachel looked back once, scanning the dock. For a heartbeat she thought she saw him — the bowler hat cocked at that familiar angle, the broad shoulders that had darkened so many doorways. Her throat closed, the air caught sharp in her chest. But when she blinked, the shape was gone, or never there at all.

The steamer groaned, shuddered, and lurched forward. The dock began to slide away, the river taking them with it. Rachel pressed her lips to Evie's hair and told herself there was no turning back.

The days blurred. The cabin reeked of damp wood and coal smoke. At night Rachel lay awake, listening to the creak of timbers and the muffled thrum of the engines; each sound felt like a warning about the future. Evie slept easily beside her, a soft glow about her face as though the lamplight lingered there longer than anywhere else.

Once, another passenger stopped Rachel in the passageway.

"Your daughter," the woman said, tilting her head curiously. "She has an old soul. You can see it in her eyes."

Rachel smiled politely, but her skin prickled.

The world on the Mississippi felt like water and motion — mornings blurred by haze, afternoons heavy with heat, nights sharp with the scent of river silt. The slow days on the river, and the waiting for whatever life lay ahead, made two or three weeks stretch into something far longer.

During those long hours on deck, Rachel thought back to the life she'd left behind in Pittsburgh — the bruises that no longer faded, the nights spent rigid in her chair, praying for kindness instead of rage. And she remembered the night she fled: his sway in the doorway, the sharp stench of alcohol, Evie's small voice saying "Pappa?" before his hand struck out like a whip. Rachel had scooped the girl up and run, ribs burning where his fist had caught her.

Sometimes Evie broke the silence. "Maybe they'll take care of us," she said softly. Rachel wasn't sure who she meant — the Lord, the captain, the water that moved like a slow-breathing chest.

Evie pointed at nothing Rachel could see. "They're waving," the girl said.

"Who, baby?"

"The ladies on the water." Evie's voice was matter-of-fact.

The days passed with a strange sameness — rain, then sun, then another low mist creeping in. Laundry flapped from the rails like faded flags. A deckhand swore the river was deeper this year, meaner. Evie, untouched by the tedium, took to the deck like a cat in sun. She would tilt her head and announce things a beat before they happened — the horn, the bend, the pelicans rising dumb and holy from the water. Once she hummed a melody that made the hairs on Rachel's neck lift.

"Where did you learn that?" Rachel asked.

"They sing it under the boat," Evie said, as if the answer lived there with the driftwood and the silt.

On some evenings, the sky turned a bruised violet and the water answered with light, slick as mercury. Others slept, lulled by the rhythm, but Rachel felt the river watching. The current seemed to know every secret she had tried to drown.

Her dreams changed too. At first, only flashes — ripples forming faces, skirts brushing the wake. Then one night, the river flattened to glass. Women walked beside the hull, their skirts spreading like wings. They turned their faces to her — pale, watchful, endless in number. Some were bruised, some weary, yet their mouths moved in unison. One held out a rosary strung not with beads but with smooth, gray stones. She could not hear their words, but when she woke, there was grit in her palm and a crescent of damp on the sheet shaped like a thumbprint.

The steamer kept its course. A veil of vapor drifted through the decks, clinging to the railings like lace. The crew began to move quieter, as though sound offended the river. Even laughter sounded wrong, too sharp, too human.

By afternoon on their final stretch, the air thickened again; a fine mist braided the rails. It smelled faintly of lilies left too long in a vase. Rachel swallowed the taste and kept her eyes on the seam where water met sky, as if reading a line meant only for her.

Toward journey's end, a heavy shroud of vapor rolled across the water. Rachel thought she saw him again — the tilt of a hat, a shadow among the passengers. Her stomach dropped. She turned quickly, but she couldn't see his familiar face among the people on board.

At dawn, the murk unstitched itself. Spires came first, then iron lace catching droplets like dew on a web. Balconies grew from the damp as though the city had been seeded there and coaxed up by heat.

New Orleans sounded busy without hurrying. Bells, a cart wheel clattering, the hush of a broom against stone. A horn somewhere tested two notes, then thought better of it.

Rachel's breath stumbled. The air pressed a warm palm over her mouth and held it there, not cruel, just sure. For a heartbeat she thought she might faint, and then Evie's small weight leaned into her side, anchoring.

"Pretty," Evie said, the word bright and unafraid.

It did not look like any place Rachel had known. It looked like a story already half told, expecting her to pick up the thread. The river shouldered the hull toward the wharf. A pelican glided low and slow, then rose, lifting the morning with it.

As the gangplank thudded, Rachel felt the softest tug behind her knees, the sensation of stepping over a threshold. Not into safety; into something with a pulse.

Rachel pressed her cheek to Evie's hair and knew she was crossing into a different kind of life.

The docks pressed close with noise and heat, the air thick with salt, sweat, and spice. Men shouted over crates, gulls screamed overhead, and the river slapped against the pilings with the insistence of something that never truly released what it held. Rachel clutched Evie's hand as they stepped down the gangplank, her legs unsteady after so many days afloat.

Her brother was waiting, collar stiff, expression caught between welcome and reproach.

"Rachel," Father Michael said, gathering her into an embrace that felt more duty than warmth. He blessed Evie with a touch to her forehead, lips moving silently. "You are safe now. God has delivered you here."

But Rachel felt no safety. The city itself seemed to watch her — shutters cracked open as she passed, shadows slipping across balconies, a thousand unseen eyes tracking her steps.

The air clung to her skin, sweet and spoiled, and even the cobblestones seemed to hum faintly underfoot.

Her brother's rectory stood behind the church, a narrow building of pale brick that trapped the heat and held the scent of incense and wax. Inside, the walls were bare except for crucifixes and faded saints, their painted faces cracked and watchful. The stillness should have been holy, but it felt like something waiting to be disturbed.

That first night, Rachel found herself listening to the house breathe — the low groan of settling wood, the soft tick of cooling lamps, the distant murmur of the Quarter outside. Once she thought she heard water trickling beneath the floor, though the nearest well was half a block away.

In the mornings, she knelt beside her brother in the pews, more out of duty to him than devotion to any unseen God. The prayers felt hollow in her mouth, words worn smooth by a thousand other tongues. She bowed her head because he expected it, because it was easier than explaining that faith had abandoned her long before she fled Pittsburgh.

If God watched over the world, what kind of God built men like her husband and called them head of the household? What sort of mercy demanded she stay and be struck again and again, yet condemned her for running? Michael's sermons about sin and redemption only deepened her unease; his certainty sounded cruel, a comfort for men who'd never needed saving from one of their own.

Evie, as always, slept peacefully, her face lit by some invisible glow. Father Michael said grace for them each morning and encouraged repentance. He did not speak her husband's name, but she heard it in every silence, in every verse about forgiveness.

In the days that followed, Rachel tried to settle into the rhythm of the rectory. She helped with the washing, kept her eyes lowered, and waited for the air to feel still. It never did. The shutters rattled on windless afternoons, and sometimes, when she stood in the courtyard, she swore the stones beneath her feet shifted slightly, as though the river had found a way to run under the city itself.

She knew he would come — she felt it in her bones, the way one senses a storm long before the sky darkens.

By the week's end, the walls of the rectory felt too close. The air hung heavy with incense and unspoken things, and Rachel found excuses to step outside — errands for candles, bread, or vegetables, anything that might let her breathe.

The streets were a fever of color and noise. Market women called from beneath striped awnings, their baskets brimming with peppers and okra slick with dew. A band of children chased one another through the stalls, laughter sharp as bells. Somewhere, a man played a fiddle so low it seemed to rise from the cobblestones themselves.

Rachel pulled Evie close, though the child didn't seem afraid. If anything, she looked content — as though she already knew these sounds and smells, the rhythm of a city that pulsed like blood.

She caught fragments of language she didn't understand, charms whispered over fruit, beads clinking in a merchant's hand. Religion here was not her brother's cold altar and Latin prayers; it was alive, sweaty, fragrant with oil and flowers. A woman in a red scarf met her gaze and smiled. "You new here, chère?" she asked.

Rachel nodded before she could think. The woman's eyes, dark and kind, lingered on Evie. "Pretty little girl. She got light around her. You keep her close."

"Thank you," Rachel managed, but when she turned, the woman was already gone, swallowed by the crowd.

As they walked back toward the church, the air grew dense, humid with afternoon. Rachel felt the first drop of rain before she saw the clouds — large and warm as tears. Somewhere a bell tolled.

"Is it going to storm?" Evie asked.

"Soon."

But the storm that gathered wasn't just in the sky. Each day, Rachel felt it nearer — a pressure at the base of her throat, a weight behind her ribs. Shadows lengthened strangely at dusk, stretching toward her even when the sun was still high. Once, she looked up to the gallery above and saw a man's outline in the ironwork: a hat brim, broad shoulders. When she blinked, the shape dissolved into the lattice.

That night, she tried to pray, kneeling beside the bed. The words tangled before they left her mouth. The house exhaled slowly, as though it had been holding its breath.

"Are you listening?" she whispered into the dark. It wasn't clear whether she meant God, or the river, or something older that had begun to stir in the corners of her mind.

No answer came — only the sound of water somewhere far below, sliding through unseen channels beneath the city.

The letter arrived folded neat as prayer, its paper softened at the edges from being handled too often. The handwriting was his — careful, almost tender — the same hand that had once traced circles on her wrist before it became a fist.

Father Michael laid it beside her breakfast plate. "From home," he said, too evenly, his eyes already turned away.

She reached for it, but the seal was broken. A faint tremor passed through her.

"You read it?"

He hesitated. "I was concerned for your soul, Rachel. You left a marriage; the Church must guide you back to what is right."

Her throat went dry. "You had no right."

"It is my duty," he said. "And his words—"

"His *words*?"

Michael lifted the paper. "He sounds repentant. He admits his faults. You know as well as I that men may fall into sin, but God's grace restores them. It is a wife's place to forgive."

Rachel stared at him, barely hearing the clatter of dishes from the kitchen. The same old refrain, wrapped in scripture like a noose.

"Did God also make his fists?" she asked quietly. "Did He bless them before they struck me?"

Her brother's mouth tightened. "Don't blaspheme. He is your husband. You took vows before the Lord."

The sound that escaped her was half-laugh, half-sob. "The Lord," she said. "The Lord made men like him and priests like you, and calls that justice."

She took the letter from his hand and carried it into the courtyard. The sun pressed hard, bright enough to sting. Evie played nearby, tracing shapes in the dust with a twig, humming under her breath.

The first lines trembled as she read them aloud, her voice flat.

My dearest Rachel, it began. *I have had time to think. I was not myself when you left — the drink, the grief, the loneliness — all of it confused me. A man can lose his way, but the Lord teaches us to forgive. I know your heart, and I know you would not wish our child to grow up without her father. Come home and all will be well. I've set aside the bottle. I've prayed for your soul and mine.*

The words were meant to soothe, yet they scraped like glass. He knew exactly which tones to strike — remorse, piety, reason. The voice she had once believed.

You will see I've changed, he wrote. *A wife should not live apart from her husband; it gives the wrong impression. People talk, Rachel. Come home and we can start again, as God intended.*

When she reached the end, her vision blurred with fury. She tore the page once, then again, the sound crisp as breaking ice.

Her brother's voice came from the doorway. "Rachel," he said, gentler now, as though speaking to a stubborn parishioner. "Anger won't save you. Pride won't, either. Go home while there's still a chance for grace."

She turned, shaking. "If that's grace, I want none of it."

The paper hissed as it burned, the ink blistering into black curls. The smoke rose sharp and bitter, sweetened by ink and something else — something faintly metallic, as though the river itself had caught the scent.

Evie looked up. "Is it from him?"

"It was," Rachel said.

She carried the dish outside and scattered the ash into the garden. The fragments lifted, caught in the humid air, and drifted toward the river.

Inside, the house gave a long, settling creak. The crucifixes on the wall seemed to tilt, as if the saints had turned to watch.

Rachel stood in the doorway, her anger cooling into something steadier. He had said all the right things before — every morning after the shouting, the broken glass, the sting of his hand. *I'm sorry, I didn't mean it. You know I love you. I'll stop drinking, you'll see.* Each apology had come with the same soft voice, the same trembling hands, the same promise to change. She had lost count of them all, but this time the words no longer reached her.

She looked toward the dark stretch of the river, where the ashes had vanished. "He won't reach us here," she murmured — though she couldn't tell if she meant the man, or the God her brother served.

The days that followed carried a brittle quiet, like the air before rain. Father Michael spoke to her less; when he did, his words were wrapped in scripture sharp enough to draw blood. She could feel his disappointment at every meal, every silence that settled between the clink of dishes.

On the second morning after the letter, he left early for the parish and did not return until nightfall. When he did, he brought with him a stiffness that hadn't been there before. "I've written to him," he said simply. "Your husband deserves to know you are safe."

Rachel's stomach dropped. "You had no right."

"I have every right," he answered, though his voice stayed maddeningly calm. "He is your husband. He seeks forgiveness. You should be grateful that he still wishes to make amends."

She wanted to shout, to strike the table, to break the calm that made his cruelty seem holy. Instead, she rose from her chair and left the room, her hands trembling.

That night, sleep refused her. The house seemed alive with small movements — the creak of beams, the sigh of air against the shutters. Each sound pressed against her chest like a warning. When she finally dozed, she dreamed of footsteps in water, slow and deliberate, coming closer.

By dawn, she knew she could not stay. The rectory felt less like shelter and more like a cell, her brother's prayers turning the air thick as incense. He would hand her back as easily as he passed a chalice from one pair of hands to another.

At breakfast, he asked if she'd prayed for guidance.
"I have," she said. "And I think I've been answered."

He smiled faintly, mistaking her meaning. "Then you'll do what's right."

"Yes," she said, and finished her coffee with shaking fingers.

All that day she moved through the rooms as if through water, her mind turning over possibilities — the docks, the markets, the old women who spoke softly to Evie as they passed. She would find a way to disappear before he came.

But as evening deepened, the air changed. A heaviness settled through the rectory, thick and close, as though the city itself had stopped to listen. From somewhere beyond the churchyard came the faint toll of a bell, out of step with the hour.

Evie looked up from her meal. "Momma," she said, her voice small but certain. "He's coming."

Rachel froze. The spoon slipped from her fingers, clattering against the plate.

Later, when the last light had drained from the windows, she began to pack the few things she owned—Evie's dress, a loaf of bread wrapped in cloth, a small tin of coins. She meant to leave before full dark, though she hadn't decided where. The markets, perhaps. Somewhere near the river. Somewhere the church could not find her.

The knock came just as she tied the bundle shut—three firm raps that made the walls tremble.

Voices murmured in the front room: her brother's low and steady, another roughened by travel.

She froze. The sound of boots on the wooden floor made her stomach twist.

When she entered, Father Michael stood beside the man she had fled. Her husband's hat rested politely in his hands; his face was clean-shaven, his eyes soft with the same practiced sorrow she had seen so many mornings after.

"Rachel," Michael said, relief and pride tangled in his tone. "He's come to take you home."

Her husband nodded. "Your brother told me where you were. I only want what's right, Rach. You were frightened, that's all." His voice gentled, a caress made of habit. "You know me."

She stared at him, the words catching behind her teeth. "Yes," she said finally. "I do."

He took a step closer, reaching for her hand. "It can be as it was."

Her laugh broke out before she could stop it. "That's what frightens me most."

Michael's brow furrowed. "Rachel, please. He's repented. You can't throw away a marriage because of anger."

She turned to her brother, astonished. "Because of anger? You read his letter. You saw what he—"

Her husband moved quicker than memory. The back of his hand struck her cheek with a sharp, wet sound. The blow spun her halfway around. Evie screamed from the stairs.

Father Michael's mouth opened but no sound came. He looked from Rachel's bleeding lip to the man beside him, horror dawning too late.

Rachel touched her cheek, the skin already swelling, and something inside her snapped loose. She grabbed Evie's hand. "We're leaving."

Her husband lunged. "You're not running again."

But she was already out the door, dragging Evie behind her. The night air hit like fire, thick with jasmine and rot. The streets of the Quarter blurred around them—balconies, lanterns, the flash of a horse's flank. Behind, his boots struck the stones, steady and close.

They ran until the rectory's bells were lost behind them, until the narrow streets opened into the wide breath of Jackson Square. The cathedral loomed ahead, its pale spires rising through the humid dark like candles left burning too long. Rachel stopped beneath the oaks, her chest tight, breath tearing through her throat.

He was there at the edge of the square — hat gone, hair plastered to his forehead with sweat. His voice was low, almost tender, the way it always began. "Rachel. You don't have to make this harder. Come back. We can start over. I've changed."

She backed away, pulling Evie close. Her face twisted, "You just proved you have not."

"I've prayed. I swear it. We belong together. Don't turn people against me, Rach. You know how they talk."

The same words, the same rhythm — soft enough to pass for love until it curdled. "You should go," she said.

He took a step toward her, hands open. "Come on now. Let's stop this foolishness."

Evie's fingers tightened in hers. "Momma," the child whispered. "They're here."

Rachel blinked. "Who?"

"The ladies from the river."

A shiver ran through the air, as if the whole city exhaled. The scent of jasmine and wet stone thickened. Somewhere close, a door slammed, then another. The cathedral bells began to toll, wild and unsummoned, their sound rolling like thunder across the square.

Her husband's face twisted. "What is this?"

Rachel turned her head. The balconies that ringed the square were no longer empty. Women stood there, dozens of them — faint outlines, skirts lifting in a wind that wasn't there. Their faces were pale, eyes endless. The same women she had dreamed of, the same who had walked the river beside the boat.

He stepped back, his voice breaking. "What trick—"

Evie lifted her chin, her blue eyes catching what light remained. "They don't like what you did," she said softly, bitterly.

Rachel felt warmth spread through her chest, not fear but something steadier, older. The air shimmered; the shadows leaned forward. She met his gaze and just knew. "It's over," she said, her voice calm at last.

The women's whispers rose, soft but unstoppable — the sound of wind moving through reeds, of water speaking its own language.

He spun in place, searching for someone solid to blame, for logic to fasten onto. "Stop it," he barked, though his voice was already fraying. "You hear me? Stop this."

No one moved. The air itself seemed to thicken, trembling with quiet fury. The hem of his coat stirred though there was no breeze. From the balconies, the pale faces leaned a little closer, eyes dark and endless as the river.

"Rachel," he said, the word breaking against his teeth. "Make it stop."

She didn't answer.

He took a step back, then another, his boots skidding on wet stone. The brim of his hat slipped from his grasp and landed upside down, collecting rain. His gaze darted toward the cathedral — toward sanctuary — but the doors had closed. A streak of lightning flared, and for an instant the square seemed full of water again, the women gliding over it as they had in her dreams.

He let out a strangled sound, half curse, half plea, and turned to run. His figure lurched down the alley, swallowed by shadow, the echo of his footsteps swallowed too.

Silence followed, thick with the smell of rain.

Evie slipped her hand into Rachel's. "He can't hurt us anymore," she said, her tone almost gentle, as if explaining something obvious.

Rachel looked up at the cathedral, its windows flickering with candlelight. She did not know if he had fled or if the city had claimed him. Only that New Orleans had chosen her.

Scent of Shadows and Roses

Her mother had named her Autumn because it was the season that burned brightest before the world fell quiet. It was celebration and surrender in one breath. Stella would hold up a leaf to the light and marvel at how the veins made a map of fire—gold folded into copper, copper brooding into red. Even brown, so often dismissed as mud or cardboard, she defended with almost holy fervor. Brown was velvet chocolate and polished mahogany, cherry wood in the afternoon sun, the deep swirl of coffee before the first sip. When Autumn thought of brown now, she didn't see dullness at all. She saw her mother's long, wavy hair slipping over her shoulders, warmth living in her eyes, and the flash of white teeth in a smile bright enough to tilt a room toward joy.

Wind chimes stirred in the courtyard behind the shop. They never sounded quite in tune, as if the breeze carried its own discordant hand across their metal ribs. A small draft breathed in under the back door, bearing the mingle of roses, gardenias, and jasmine—too much for so small a space, and yet always right, like a dress inherited from someone beloved and just your size. The fragrance coiled up her spine, memory stirring in her blood. She allowed herself ten heartbeats of drifting, ten beats in which grief loosened its fingers.

"A dozen roses. Red ones. And a card."

The voice split the reverie. Autumn blinked toward the counter and found a man framed in the door's pale light.

"Red roses for love and passion," she said, slipping on a smile that felt like a glove she hadn't worn in months. "Someone special?"

He might have been carved from dusk. Hair the color of burnished copper caught the lamp's weak glow; the lines of his jaw were decisive without seeming cruel. But it was his eyes she couldn't stop staring at—gray with a strike of green, like sea-glass dredged up after a storm. That gaze held steady without leaning forward. It watched and waited, as if the truth might step forward on its own.

A small flicker moved in Autumn's chest, so swift she mistrusted it. Attraction, unwelcome as a thorn snagging silk. She flattened it with habit. That door had been locked since Stella's last breath, and nothing good would come of opening it for a stranger with storm-colored eyes.

"Yes," he said finally, voice pitched low, as if speech were a thing to be used sparingly. "Someone important."

"Sometimes yellow roses are better," Autumn heard herself say, though she had no idea why. He hadn't said anything about needing forgiveness, but the words slipped out anyway, honest and uninvited.

He looked up, eyes widening — just for a second — before his expression settled again. "You're right," he said finally. "Yellow, then."

Something unreadable passed through his face, a cloud crossing behind glass. He inclined his head.

She wrapped the bouquet without speaking further. Once,

long ago and far away, yellow petals meant suspicion, jealousy. Later, the meaning was softened to apology. Flowers were stubborn creatures—no matter how people revised their language, the old shadows clung. She tied ribbon, slipped in a blank card, and offered the arrangement over the counter. When he took it, his fingers brushed the air near hers. No contact, only the sense of a winter's day and standing very close to a window where the sun had found a way in.

The bell rang as the door shut behind him, leaving the shop oddly hollow. Business had been poor. After Stella's death, almost everything had been poor. Still, Autumn did not regret telling him the truth about the roses, but her impulsive decision to do so still confused her.

One hour until closing. One hour until the long bolt drew across the back door, and she could step into the courtyard—the sanctuary that bloomed out of reason, the place her mother's touch had once made endless.

When the last customer had gone and the till lay balanced to the cent, she turned out the lights one by one. The darkness felt clean as water. She slid the bolt and stepped into the garden.

The air changed. Coolness pressed its palm to her forehead; the smell of damp earth climbed her ribs. The fountain at the garden's heart whispered its strange, small language. A stone goddess rose from its center, the water forever tracing her skin, arms lifted towards the sky. Moonlight found the shallow of her palm and pooled there, as though time were a liquid easily captured.

Autumn's gaze went to the roses, as it always did. This had been her mother's true work. The hothouse roses in the shop were flowers; the ones here were a covenant. They bowed to nothing. They did not wilt, or fade, or fall. Seasons passed, storms tore through, and still they bloomed — untouched by time or weather, as though decay had simply forgotten them. Their perfume was heavy enough to linger in her hair, to haunt the air itself. Pink as blushing porcelain, yellow as wheat beneath noon, ivory white that glowed like bone in the dim, and a lavender Stella had once smuggled from Australia, swearing to protect it like a child. It had always been this way, and Autumn had always known better than to call it natural.

"Some things grow best when they're loved properly," Stella had said once, and closed the subject with a smile that brooked no questions. Love was the spell, then. Or love held the spell's key. When Stella laughed, the garden seemed to breathe; when she wept, the roses dimmed for her. It had felt easy when she had been here, love moving through the courtyard like one more scent.

Now the garden was Autumn's, and the secret of the forever roses had been buried with her mother, heart to root.

Autumn made a slow circle of the fountain, fingers skimming leaves and petals. She whispered the way she always did, not a prayer exactly, not a spell, but something that made the air thicken as if listening. Somewhere, she liked to think, Stella tilted her head and heard.

Something in her stilled when she reached the red roses. The bush had softened its spine. Blooms sagged as if exhausted after a long vigil. Petals loosened with the weariness of the old and dropped one by one into the soil—dark as blood, soft as velvet, already turning toward ruin. The perfume had changed too. Sweetness remained, but it was the sweetness of a cupboard that had kept bread too long.

Autumn looked up without meaning to. The goddess watched, moon cupped in her stone hand. There had always been something unnerving about the statue. Tonight there was a hint of judgment in the calm.

She went to her knees in the dirt without a care for damaging her dress. A fallen petal collapsed under her fingertip. A sob swelled, scorching the back of her throat.
Stella's roses had never withered. Not here.
Not ever.

She stayed there long after the night had emptied itself of sound, until grief softened into a kind of silence. At some point, she made her way to her bed. Sleep came to her by accident in the brittle hours before dawn and left her untouched. When she opened her eyes, the scent of roses was in her hair and the taste of iron rested behind her teeth. She sat on the bed's edge in yesterday's dress and did not know where to put her hands. It felt as if the courtyard had put roots through the walls and woven itself around her bones.

By opening time, she had gathered herself into the shape of someone who swept floors, turned keys, and filled buckets. The stems stood in their tin pails—brave, thin things, like soldiers pretending their armor still held. She kept her back to the courtyard gate. There was work to do, and she resisted the pull to look at the rose bush. Not while there were flowers to sell. Not while she could still pretend the red bush had been a mistake, something dreamed and best forgotten.

The bell over the door startled her; it was nearly closing time.

"Back so soon?" Too bright. She forced a smile.

"I thought I should thank you." His voice carried that same careful economy. "The yellow roses worked. My mother liked them."

"Your mother?" The picture she'd imagined—tight-lipped wife, suspicious lover—crumbled. Shame crowded her tongue.

"She's unwell," he said, not unkindly but as if stating the weather. "We're not good at speaking. The flowers filled the silence."

Autumn's hands loosened on the counter. "I'm glad they helped," she said, and meant it so much that the words ached on the way out.

He inclined his head. "What would you suggest next time?" His tone was careful, almost clinical.

"Maybe not flowers," she heard herself say before she'd even thought it through. "Something that lasts. Something that keeps on living."

He shifted, a hand half-way to his coat pocket, when something slipped free from his cuff and fell beside the register.

A petal.

Not yellow.

Red—deep as a pulse, rich with perfume that didn't belong to any bloom in the shop.

Autumn's heart stumbled, then found itself running. She knew that scent the way she knew her mother's footsteps on the stairs. It lived only in the courtyard's red bush.

Her gaze lifted. He followed the look and saw the petal as if for the first time. He brushed it aside with one finger. The gesture could have been careless. The corner of his mouth claimed a shadow of a smile.

"Strange," he said, almost companionably. "Perhaps it followed me."

The petal lay between them, cool and damning. The garden had sent it like a sealed letter. The message was not written for her alone.

A breath of air pressed against the bolted door. Then another—harder. The latch rattled.

Autumn turned toward it, pulse quickening. "Excuse me a moment. Please wait here," she murmured.

The door shuddered, then swung open on its own, spilling humid night into the room. The scent of the red roses flooded in—heady, urgent, impossible to ignore.

He stepped back instinctively, eyes narrowing. "Is that—?"

She didn't answer. The perfume pulled her forward, past the counter and through the open door. The courtyard waited, breathing.

Outside, the Quarter pressed humid and noisy—laughter scraped with heat, insects arguing at the edge of hearing. Inside the courtyard the air grew denser, cool as a cellar. Roses climbed the walls as though the building itself were the trellis. Pale blooms held moonlight like lanterns cupped in both hands. The fountain whispered, and the goddess did not blink.

She crossed to the red bush. Petals lay strewn as if a great crimson bird had been plucked where it stood. The bush breathed a tired perfume, and all she could think was: Everything tires eventually, even a miracle.

"Mum," she said, too softly for anyone but a ghost to hear. "What am I meant to do? You never told me how."

Water shifted on stone. Moonlight pooled deeper in the goddess's hand. Stella had always cleaned that statue with a cloth dipped in milk and whispered to it under her breath, as if the stone remembered language. Autumn had laughed once. Stella had let her laugh and gone on with the cloth.

A hush moved the roses like a small wind. Something brushed Autumn's ear that wasn't wind and wasn't her hair.

It isn't the roses, Autumn. It's you. Love keeps them alive. But love cannot grow behind locked doors.

Stella's voice, low as the bottom note of a lullaby. Or memory dressed in her voice. It made no difference to the way

Autumn's body answered. She pressed her hands to her eyes. "I don't know how."

Then learn, said the hush. *Let it in.*

The roses held their breath, or made her think they did. Perfume thickened until it was almost food. Somewhere in the alley, a cat sent something clattering and swore in its own language.

The rest of the city stepped back a pace. The courtyard waited.

A shift in the air made her turn. He was there—close enough that she could feel the shape of his presence before she heard him move.

"I thought I asked you to wait." The words came out sharper than she intended, the edge of fear hidden beneath the command.

He took a step forward, hesitant but certain of his reason. "I tried," he said. "But something about this place—about you—it won't let me go. The scent..." His voice faltered as he glanced toward the red bush. "It's everywhere. Down the street. In my rooms. I couldn't stay away. It's intoxicating—and it feels as if it's calling me."

She searched his face for mockery and found none. The moon caught in the gray-green of his eyes, and the garden seemed to breathe between them.

A single red petal clung to the seam of his sleeve, trembling as though still attached to the failing bloom.

Her mother's voice filled her head again, not soft this time. *Let it in.*

Her chest ached from everything she'd kept locked away. Since Stella, her life had been ritual and quiet, safe but small. The roses had fed on her grief, and now they wanted what she denied herself—love, and the risk of it.

Her eyes met his fully. The gray and green were not simple. They made a depth, and depth made places to hide. He did not look away.

She reached for the red bush. Her fingers found a bloom that had begun to fall toward itself, and she touched it as if she might split it further. Instead, warmth moved under her skin the way a remembered word moves through the mouth. The petals took on weight. Color drew itself in deeper, richer. One by one the heads lifted from their exhaustion. A murmur went through the roses like a shiver of wings before flight.

The enchantment unfolded as if it had been waiting all night for her hand, for the warmth she'd kept from it too long.

Autumn put a shaking hand to her breastbone. The truth was simple enough to frighten her. The roses would go on only if she did—if she dared to live as fiercely as they had bloomed for her mother. If she opened the door she'd kept closed for so long. If she stopped tending her grief as though it could survive on tears alone.

He stepped closer. The petal on his sleeve stayed with him as if loyalty were a thing fabric could feel.

He lifted his hand, slow and uncertain—an offering, not a request.

Autumn's breath caught. Her hand rose instinctively to stop him, then hesitated in the space between them. *Let it in,* her mother's voice murmured. *Let him in.*

She let her hand fall. His fingers brushed her cheek—lightly, reverently—as though afraid the moment itself might break.

They stood that way, saying nothing. The roses breathed around them, their scent deepening until it seemed to pulse with the night. Moonlight pooled at their feet. Somewhere, the fountain whispered, steady as breath, and the goddess watched from her place above, her stone face glimmering with quiet approval.

The roses lifted higher, scent swelling, as if the garden itself exhaled relief.

A Light for the Lost

The boy's hands smelled of sulphur and smoke, his fingers nicked from striking matches all evening. Melbourne's streets were a patchwork of gold and shadow, gas lamps blooming one by one as the sun bled out behind the roofs.

He hurried through the wider streets, where couples strolled and hansom cabs clattered past, but slowed when he reached the laneways. Narrow, brick-walled, and echoing with their own kind of silence, they seemed to swallow the light whole.

One lamp in particular gave him trouble.

It stood crooked at the bend of an alley, its glass blackened with soot, the post leaning like a tired man. No matter how many times he coaxed the flame, it sputtered, hissed, and died. Tonight was no different. He lit the wick; it flared, then guttered out.

The boy frowned, striking another match. The flame trembled as though some invisible breath leaned close and blew.

He shivered.

His master had warned him about this one. "Don't linger there," the old man had muttered, eyes on his boots. "That laneway's got its own company."

The boy hadn't asked what he meant. He wasn't sure he wanted to know.

Still, he tried again. The match flared, smoke curling around his hands. For an instant the alley lit up, bricks glowing red, shadows sharp.

And in that instant, he thought he heard the faint tread of footsteps behind him, too light to be a man's, too close to be imagined.

He spun, the flame sputtering in the draft.

The alley lay empty.

But the feeling of being watched pressed close, as steady as the dark.

The boy held the match until it singed his fingers, then shook it out. Smoke curled upward, vanishing into the dark.

He told himself to move on, to finish his round before his master scolded him for dawdling. Yet something rooted him there, a prickle in the air like the moment before rain.

Another sound stirred — not footsteps this time, but the faint scrape of cloth against brick. He froze, listening.

"Hello?" His voice came out too loud, breaking the hush.

A pause. Then, from the bend of the laneway, a figure eased into the lightless space. A girl, no older than he was, her dress plain and hem frayed, hair loose about her shoulders.

She stopped a few paces away, head tilted.

"I thought you were gone," she said softly.

The boy frowned. "Gone where?"

Her eyes flicked toward the unlit lamp. "It's always dark here. Always." She stepped closer, her shoes making no sound on the cobbles. "But you've got matches. Could you—would you walk me out?"

The boy swallowed, fingers curling tight around his box of matches. Something about her voice unsettled him — not unkind, but far away, like hearing someone speak across water.

Still, he found himself nodding. "If you like."

The girl's mouth curved in the faintest smile.

And as she drifted nearer, the lamp behind him guttered once more, as though refusing to burn in her presence.

They set off side by side, though the boy kept a pace behind, the box of matches clutched against his chest. The laneway pressed close around them, brick walls sweating damp, the air sharp with the tang of horse dung from the main street beyond.

"You work the lamps," she said after a silence, her voice light, curious.

He nodded. "Apprentice. My master does the big streets. I get these."

"These," she echoed, glancing at the crooked post they'd left behind. "It never stays lit, does it?"

He stopped. "How'd you know that?"

The girl didn't answer right away. Her eyes roved the shadows, as if searching for something that wasn't there. "I've been here before," she said at last. "A long time. I keep thinking I'll find my way home, but the alleys all twist. Every corner turns me back."

The boy frowned. "Where d'you live?"

She smiled faintly, the expression strange and sad. "Near enough. But when I go to look, the house is never there."

Her words made his skin prickle. He almost spoke, almost told her she was talking nonsense, but something in her face stopped him. The sadness in it was too real.

They turned another bend. The faint outlines of the coffee palace rose ahead, its windows glowing pale against the night. The boy glanced up at the rows of curtained glass, comforted by the thought of people inside—travelers drinking coffee, families asleep in warm beds.

But one window was bare. And in its square of light stood a man, still as a carving. His eyes fixed on the street below, his hands braced on the sill.

The boy stopped short. "Someone's watching."

The girl only sighed. "He always is."

The boy shifted uneasily, his gaze fixed on the figure in the window. The man hadn't moved, hadn't blinked. Just staring, as though he'd been carved into the building itself.

"Who is he?" the boy asked, his voice dropping to a whisper.

The girl's eyes flicked upward, then away again. "A guest. He checked in long ago and never left."

The boy frowned. "That's daft. Nobody lives in a coffee palace."

Her smile was quick and brittle. "No one lives in a laneway either. Not really."

The words slid cold down his spine. He wanted to argue, to tell her she was wrong, but the way she walked—light as dust, her steps making no sound—held him quiet.

At the corner, the wind rose. The lamp they'd left sputtered once more, then flared, a pale bloom against the dark. The boy turned, startled, but the girl only closed her eyes as though soothed by it.

"It never burned for me before," she said softly. "Not since..." Her voice caught.

He stared at her, heart thudding. "Since when?"

She met his gaze then, and for a fleeting instant he saw it: the mud-smeared hem of her dress, the crushed leather of a shoe, the faint mark of reins across her arm. A dray horse, heavy and blind in the dark, and a girl who hadn't moved fast enough.

The vision blinked away, but the boy's breath came sharp.

The girl looked down at her hands, twisting them as though they still hurt. "I think," she whispered, "I've been waiting for the light."

The boy stole another glance at the window. The man hadn't moved, hadn't blinked. Just staring, his face caught in the pale glow like a fly trapped in amber.

"Why does he watch?" the boy asked, his voice barely more than breath.

The girl walked with her head bowed, fingers worrying at the frayed hem of her dress. "Because he can't look away."

"From what?"

Her eyes flicked toward the cobbles, then to the crooked lamp they'd left behind. "From here. From me."

The boy frowned. "You know him?"

Her lips pressed thin. "He drove a cart. A big dray horse pulling barrels for the coffee palace kitchens. He came through the lane too fast. It wasn't his fault, not really—the horse spooked at something—but..." She stopped, swallowing hard.

The boy waited, his chest tight.

"I am small," she said finally, voice breaking into a whisper. "And the wheels were so wide."

For a moment the laneway tilted, shadows swimming around them. The boy saw the scene in a flash: the girl stumbling, the horse rearing, the man shouting, pulling the reins until his arms shook. Too late.

The vision vanished, leaving the air heavy and still.

The girl stared at her hands, twisting them as though she could scrub the memory away. "He carried me here," she murmured. "He set me down by that lamp. I think he thought if someone found me quick enough..." She shook her head. "But no one did."

The boy shivered, the box of matches slick in his palm.

"And now?" he asked.

She lifted her gaze, her eyes enormous in the gloom. "Now he waits. And I wander."

The boy's throat felt tight. He wanted to run, to spill out onto the broad street where the lamps shone steady and people still lived. But something in the girl's face held him there — the weary sadness of someone who had walked this lane too long.

She stopped beneath the crooked post, the lamp above them dark as pitch. For a moment she simply looked up at it, her hair catching the faint glow from the coffee palace window.

"I think it was meant to burn for me," she said. "But it never did."

The boy struck a match. His fingers trembled as the sulphur flared, spilling light across her pale face. She flinched back, as if afraid.

"If I light it," he asked softly, "what happens?"

Her lips parted, then closed again. "I don't know."

Across the way, the man in the window shifted for the first time. His hand lifted, pressing hard against the glass. His face was a ruin of sorrow, eyes hollow, pleading.

The boy looked from him to her.

Her gaze followed his, landing on the figure above. For an instant something passed between them — not forgiveness, not accusation, just the weight of a truth that bound them both.

The match burned down, searing his fingertips. He hissed and shook it out.

The girl didn't move. She only whispered, "Please."

Her gaze followed his, landing on the figure above. For an instant something passed between them — not forgiveness, not accusation, just the weight of a truth that bound them both.

The match burned down, searing his fingertips. He hissed and shook it out.

The girl didn't move. She only whispered, "Please."

The boy pulled another match from the box, but his hand hovered. His pulse drummed in his ears. What if the light wasn't enough? What if he failed them both, left her wandering and the man still watching?

She was staring at the window. Her lips moved, forming a word he couldn't catch, before she whispered, "He couldn't live with it. He hanged himself in one of the upper rooms. I know. I saw."

The boy swallowed hard. He was only an apprentice lamplighter, yet something inside him stirred. Somehow he knew the work was never only for the living. If the man's guilt kept him staring, if the girl's sorrow kept her waiting, then perhaps the lamp had always been meant for more.

"You think the light will free you?" he asked.

Her gaze dropped to him, eyes wide and solemn. "I don't know. Only that it means something. The lamp, the darkness, the way I'm always here—waiting."

His fingers tightened around the match. The weight of it felt heavy as destiny.

He glanced up at the window. The man pressed both palms flat to the glass now, shoulders bowed, his mouth shaping words the boy couldn't hear.

The girl stood beneath the lamp, her eyes fixed on the darkened glass above. Her lips moved too. It was like they were having a conversation he wasn't privy to.

The boy's breath trembled out of him. Slowly, he struck the match.

The flame bloomed, fragile and fierce in the hollow of his hand.

He lifted it to the lamp. The wick caught, flared—and this time, it held.

The girl smiled faintly, lifted a hand in farewell, and stepped into the light. The glow wrapped her, held her—and she was gone.

The boy looked up just in time to see the man in the window. His hands slipped from the glass, his shoulders eased, and his outline thinned to nothing until the pane reflected only darkness.

He stood alone beneath the lamp, the match burned down to his fingertips, the night pressing close again. But above him the flame hummed steady, burning as it should, as if at last satisfied.

He slipped the spent match into his pocket and moved on to the next street, knowing now that a lamplighter's flame was never only for the living.

Acknowledgements

My deepest thanks to my family and friends for their patience, encouragement, and for reading early drafts of these stories with such care. Your thoughtful comments helped me shape this collection into what it is. A special thank you to Justin Mateo Gutierrez, whose stories and spirit inspired *Smoke and Rosemary*, and to Rene Bonee — whose family story inspired *Between Shadows and Saints* and whose insight sparked the idea for *Scent of Shadows and Roses*.

Ree Winter

www.smallsanctuaries.com